T5-CCV-975

A
TOR
DOUBLE
ACTION
WESTERN

**Look for Tor Double Action Westerns
from these authors**

MAX BRAND
ZANE GREY
LEWIS B. PATTEN
WAYNE D. OVERHOLSER
CLAY FISHER
FRANK BONHAM
OWEN WISTER
STEVE FRAZEE
HARRY SINCLAIR DRAGO*
JOHN PRESCOTT*
WILL HENRY*

*coming soon

Steve Frazee

LOOK BEHIND EVERY HILL
THE BIG TROUBLE

TOR

A TOM DOHERTY ASSOCIATES BOOK
NEW YORK

LOOK BEHIND EVERY HILL

Copyright © 1952 by Stadium Publishing Corporation. First published in *Complete Western Book Magazine*.

THE BIG TROUBLE

Copyright © 1953 by Stadium Publishing Corporation. First published in *Complete Western Book Magazine*.

Compilation copyright © 1990 by Tor Books.

A Tor Book
Published by Tom Doherty Associates, Inc.
49 West 24th Street
New York, N.Y. 10010

Cover art by Ballestar

ISBN: 0-812-50540-9

First edition: October 1990

Printed in the United States of America

0 9 8 7 6 5 4 3 2 1

LOOK BEHIND EVERY HILL

CHAPTER 1
Rebel

Vastness was the burden. Its silence was eloquent, promising nothing but time and defeat. From the Empire Mountains to the last dim break of the Spotted Hills, the long land miles threw their challenge at any man foolish enough to pit a plow against their lonely bigness.

Carmody Steele tried it, with his pretty wife, Faith, and his two children. His shack was an affront to the rawness. The sun hastened to brown the boards and twist them from the nails that held them, and the winter wind tried to tear the boards away.

Lee Hester said the land was fit for cattle only. He was a Northern man, like the owners of Wagonwheel, the other big ranch in the Spotted Hills. The great log ranch-house of the Hesters was in a basin at the head of Pittsburg Creek. Cloverleaf, they called it. Hester and his neighbor, miles apart, waited for Carmody Steele, the Rebel cavalryman, to starve out.

Steele's daughter was twelve; Vaughn, the son, was sixteen. Because of the women, Lee Hester said he would be patient; but he added that there was, of course, a limit to his patience.

Faith Steele was the first to break. She stayed longer and longer each visit at Mrs. Trotter's boarding house on the railroad at Gettysburg. Mrs. Trotter was a Southerner too, but she lacked a plantation upbringing, so the country did not frighten her.

A young conductor who ate every fourth day at the boarding house kept telling Faith Steele that this was a hopeless country for women. His uniform would have looked jaunty beside Carmody Steele's rough clothing, all stained with the red soil of Elk Run. One day Mrs. Steele went with the young conductor, east toward the memory of great rivers and flowers and friendly houses standing close together in countless towns and cities.

She left Nan, the girl, with Mrs. Trotter; leaving dark-browed Carmody and Vaughn to fight the red earth of Elk Run without a wife and mother. That happened on a raw spring day.

Carmody did not know about it for two days. He took Vaughn with him when he went to town to bring his daughter home. Nan was ill with grippe and Mrs. Trotter said it was best to leave her in town for another week or two. "I tried to talk her out of it, Mr. Steele." Mrs. Trotter was sincere. Her profanity startled Vaughn.

Carmody nodded. He did not look now like an ex-Confederate major. There was a sag to his body and a lumpishness about him that did not come entirely from his heavy clothes. The glory of the high-riding South was long away. Only the doggedness was left, and the breeding.

He bowed to Mrs. Trotter and thanked her. Vaughn stood silent and wondering. He was a flat-backed youth with his mother's golden complexion and his father's dark hair and eyes. All sympathy ran to his father. Betrayal.

He asked, "When is there another train East?"

Carmody smiled. He shook his head. "We'll go back to the farm, son." He always called it a farm.

He had stayed until Appomattox. He would be no different now. On the long ride home he squinted at the lonesome land. Snow still lay rotting in the shady parts of the gullies. The wind from the Empire Mountains was cold.

"You can't blame her," he said. "She grew up in a different country. There was always something around her, something at her back for reassurance. Here . . ."

Vaughn raised his head. Out here the mountains were the only thing a person could put his back against; and they seemed very far away. He had never been to them. They stood in gray and white triangles, unfriendly barriers on the long horizon.

Vaughn said, "What about Nan?"

"She'll grow up with us. She'll stay."

His father had lost one way of life, Vaughn knew. He had seen the promise of another. Maybe it was stubbornness or maybe it was determination, but Carmody Steele would stay forever on Elk Run now, if only to prove that he must have been right this second time.

Hours later the shack began to grow from a dot of yellow-streaked brown. The fields scratched on the surface of the vastness were tiny marks that could disappear after a month or so of neglect.

"Of course, some women would have stayed," Carmody said. That was the only blame he ever laid on his wife.

Lee Hester and Troutt Warner were waiting at the house. Hester was a rangy man, iron gray at the temples. There was a loose mobility about Warner's mouth, a sort of roving lewdness. His eyes were hooded at the outer corners, and the down-draping of the flesh seemed to be part of the bone structure. He and Charley Burgett owned a ranch on Pennsylvania Creek, the Wagonwheel.

Steele dismounted. He gestured toward the house. "Won't you come in?"

Hester shook his head. "We heard that you—" Hester stopped. "Your wife—" It was a delicate subject. Steele's bleak, indrawn expression did not help Hester any.

"We heard she ran out on you," Warner said.

"Yes," Steele said. It was both confirmation and a question that edged on deadly politeness.

"You won't be staying here much longer then, I suppose. The little girl and all . . ." Hester glanced at the house.

"Why, yes, I'm staying."

Warner looked at Hester. His by-passing of Steele was an insult when he said, "I told you, Lee. This waiting for nature to take its course is no good. We'll have to help him move."

"It's like this," Hester said. "We haven't got anything against you in particular, you understand." He was trying to speak with reason, Vaughn realized, perhaps because of what had happened today. Through a growing rage Vaughn realized that fact, but it served only to make him more angry.

He walked toward the house.

"Yes, you have something against me," Steele said.

Hester forgot politeness. "You're a Rebel. That, we might learn to live with, but you're planted in the middle of our land. We hoped you'd starve out. You haven't, so far. You're setting a bad example—"

Steele laughed. "That sounds familiar, considering what I saw in the South after the war. I'm setting a bad example by trying to make a living."

"Somebody else will be encouraged to move in here," Hester said. "You'd best get out, Steele."

Vaughn stood in the doorway with a rifle. "*You'd* best get out, Hester! You and Warner. Right now!"

"Put it away, son," Steele said.

Vaughn swung the rifle on Warner's chest.

"No, Vaughn," Steele said, but nothing changed and nothing happened. Across Carmody Steele's face there came the realization that authority was no longer vested in him alone. He stared at his son a moment, and then he said in a tired voice, "Yes, gentlemen, you'd better leave."

The ranchers rode away. Vaughn watched the vastness gather around them. He put the rifle

down. There was nothing here to put your back
against, nothing here that stood as a shield.

He helped his father take care of the horses,
Mitch and Corkey, good riding mounts, Steele's
only salvage from a lost war. They were not like
the lumpy team that plowed the fields. They
represented something that Steele could not
seem to find in this country, something that his
son thought he himself would never find.

The two men stood together for a moment,
looking across the raw fields.

"Maybe—" Vaughn said.

His father said, "No. We'll stay here. There
are thousands like me out here, Vaughn. The
more we run, the more we'll have to run."

Vaughn thought of the weight of all the hostility around them, hidden in the folded hills.
He had brought trouble to a point this day.

He said, "What will we do?"

"We'll cook supper. We'll do that first, and
then whatever else we have to do will come as
it will."

They brought Nan back from town the next
week. Her father told her that her mother was
not coming home, and that there was no need
to ask the question, ever.

It rode like a puzzled shock across Nan's face.
She was losing her chubby look. Her hair, rich
chestnut in color, and her long face, were sharp
reminders of Faith Steele. But her eyes were
dark, like Carmody's, and they understood a
great deal when her father spoke to her.

"You'll have to cook," Steele said. "Did
your—did you ever learn about it?"

"Not much."

"Learn now," Steele said. He spoke with unneeded harshness. Faith Steele had never been a good cook. Now it occurred to Vaughn that his father was associating that failure with other shortcomings.

"You don't scare me one little bit," Nan said. From the window of the kitchen the country was reduced considerably. Green was springing where the snow had been, and the fields seemed an important part of the whole.

That afternoon, with the red soil coming up in lumps behind the plow, Steele nodded to himself, then said, "She'll be all right, Vaughn. She's not like her mother." A little later he said, "We'll break a hundred more acres than I planned at first—there on the other side of Elk Run."

"Fine," Vaughn said. Let his father try to take his hurt out on the soil if he would.

At the far end of the field they stopped a few moments after making the turn. Carmody Steele raised one fist and said, "By God, I'll make this country bloom! I'll grow things here. You'll see."

He shook his fist at the land. Vaughn watched while the cold spring wind chilled his sweating back. The lostness of his father came to him with frightening intensity. Carmody Steele would try to lash the land because it had robbed him, because it had beaten him already.

They ate that night by a smoking lamp. The boards of the shack rattled a little under a light wind rushing from the mountains. On the windows were curtains that had once been in a mansion.

Carmody Steele stared at them. "They're too

frilly for here. I've always said that. Change them, Nan."

"There's nothing else."

"Then we'll do without." Steele went across the room and tore the curtains down. He dropped them into the woodbox. He leaned against the wall for a moment, and then he shook his head as if to clear it. He walked outside. They heard his footsteps go into the night.

"Back in Virginia grandpa used to ride his horse in the moonlight, jumping fences, when he was drunk or mad about something. Mother told me," Nan said.

Vaughn said, "He's all right. You go to bed."

Hours later Carmody returned, walking like a beaten infantryman. He sat at the kitchen table looking out on the moonlit land. The soft light shafting through the window could not hide his haggard look.

Vaughn came quietly to the doorway. "We got a lot of work to do tomorrow."

"Yes," his father answered. "Yes, I know. Did you ever walk in the moonlight, son, wondering what happens when something dies in you? No, of course you haven't. You might someday. If you're tough, Vaughn, really tough inside, you won't let anything die in you. Things change but you won't let anything die."

He rose wearily and went to bed.

They came that night in the dead still hours of slumber. Vaughn felt the house tremble. He thought it was a dream. Something snaked across the boards, as if a small animal were running on the roof. Boards groaned. The house began to move.

Outside someone said, "Downhill, you fool!"

Vaughn leaped from bed. The puncheon flooring struck him in the face. It was utter terror in the darkness for a while. There was no balance in his being. He groped and fell. Nothing in the room was where it should be.

Carmody Steele's voice came sharply. "Get the mattresses around Nan! Keep her on the floor!"

Vaughn knew now. There were men and horses outside. There were ropes on the house and it was being dragged away. He tripped on the mattress he pulled across the swaying room. He found Nan sitting in her bed. "I had a bad dream," she said. She was fully awake but did not realize it yet.

"Hang onto me, Nan." He felt her grab him hard. She knew now that she was not dreaming. He dragged her cornshuck mattress off the bed. The floor was bouncing now and everything loose was washing around the room.

The stove went over in the kitchen and threw the warm smell of soot through the darkness; and then the kitchen, an unfloored leanto, ripped from the other part of the house. Night air swooped in. Someone outside shouted, urging a horse to greater effort. In a moment the walls were creaking in. Roof boards snapped.

Vaughn was covering his sister with the second mattress, but now he picked her up and tried to stagger through the open end of the room. From outside there came the heavy rocking sound of his father's rifle. Carmody Steele had already made it through the opening.

A man cried out in alarm. The rifle replied, and then there were scattered shots and cries. The house quit moving. Vaughn put Nan on the twisted flooring, kneeling above her. The rifle boomed once more. A half dozen pistol shots replied. Some of them ripped the broken boards around Vaughn.

Some moments later the night was still, except for the sound of horses trotting in the darkness. Vaughn groped his way outside, calling his father, crying into an emptiness from which there was no echo or answer.

CHAPTER 2
"Someday I'll Kill Them All"

VAUGHN STEELE AND HIS SISTER STOOD AROUND THE cookstove, warming themselves in the gray dawn. The stove was propped up on wreckage, with a short pipe carrying its blue smoke across the chill land.

Carmody Steele was dead, lying on a mattress, covered with a second mattress. He had been dead when his son stumbled through the darkness and found him. His children stood close together at the stove not looking directly at each other.

Nan limped when she stepped away to gather an armful of board fragments for the fire.

"You hurt?" Vaughn asked.

She answered crossly. "No."

The first of the sun touched high on the Empire Mountains with a rosy glow, but here on the lonesome land the cold was sharp.

"We'd better have something to eat," Nan said, "before—we'll, we'd better have something to eat."

Vaughn poked around in the ruined house. He found enough for breakfast. When he returned with the food in a chipped graniteware pan Nan was crying. She held tight to him and sobbed, "Where's our mother, Vaughn? Why did she go away?"

They tried to comfort each other but they had no answers to give to each other. Vaughn looked over his sister's head at the mattresses on the damp ground. He thought, *Someday I'll kill every one of them. I'll get them one by one.*

While Nan cooked he cleaned the rifle, and then he turned over boards and moved broken household gear until he found a handful of cartridges. Guns and horses—Carmody Steele had loved them both. His rifle was here yet but the horses had been taken, or run off.

They had just finished burying their father in the rich red soil only a few feet from where he had died when Vaughn saw the rider coming with a packhorse. He overbore an urge to shout and wave his arms to attract the man's attention.

He knew who it was, Drake Gardner, who lived somewhere against the mountains. On his infrequent trips for supplies Gardner generally stopped a few minutes at the Steele place, seldom dismounting, saying very little before he led his packhorse on toward what Vaughn had imagined must be a mysterious existence there below the tall Empires.

The wrecked shack caught Gardner's attention. He came in faster than usual. He was what

Carmody Steele had called a young-old man, a slender fellow with eyes like chips of black stone. One side of his face was scarred and pitted as if flecks of molten iron had splashed against him.

On that side the view gave him an evil appearance; the other side was different, the face of a young man, but there were lines already growing in his cheeks and the flesh around his eyes was puckered with little spoke-like wrinkles.

He sat his horse and said nothing, seeing everything in quick, hard flicks of his black eyes. Then he swung down and walked around the grave of Carmody Steele.

"What's the matter with your ankle?" he asked Nan.

The girl shook her head, moving closer to Vaughn.

"Come here." Gardner's tone expected obedience.

The girl walked slowly around some shattered boards, holding her hands behind her back, and stopped in front of Gardner.

"Let me see that foot. Sit down there on the ground." Gardner felt the ankle gently. He removed Nan's shoe, and a moment later he stared at Vaughn. "Look here."

The girl had stepped on a nail. It had gone through her foot, leaving a tiny purplish mark on top.

"Not nearly as nice as a good clean bullet hole," Gardner said. He stood up. "Did you recognize anybody, Steele?"

Steele. The name carried stature. Vaughn shook his head. "It was dark."

"Naturally." The sun was rising. Gardner

looked around at the Spotted Hills. "Where's the horses?"

Vaughn shrugged.

"Have you looked for them?"

"Not yet."

Gardner frowned. He appeared to be facing a situation that did not bother him greatly. His face showed no sympathy for the victims, no hatred of those who had caused the ruin. If there was any expression at all on his face, it was annoyance.

"Your mother's gone back East?"

"She ran away," Vaughn said. Betrayal. It built a savageness in him, not particularly against his mother, but against all else that had happened.

"You have folks—" Gardner inclined his head toward the sun—"back there someplace?"

"Virginia," Vaughn said. "They're all scattered now, I guess."

"Yeah." Gardner seemed to understand. He pulled a bridle from a tangle of clothing wrapped around some studding. He dropped it again. "Work that foot with your hands," he said to Nan. "Squeeze it and make it bleed."

"It hurts." The girl's lips were trembling.

"Make it bleed!" Gardner frowned, annoyed. He glanced at his horse, as if he were thinking that he could mount and ride away and save himself a lot of trouble.

"What will you do now?" he asked Vaughn.

"I'll take Nan to Mrs. Trotter, and then I'll find something to do."

"Will you?" Gardner said shortly. "The big woman who runs the boardhouse, you mean?"

Vaughn nodded.

"She didn't cause any of this."

Vaughn blinked. "Of course not."

"Then why bother her with your problems? She's not quite the woman to be raising a girl anyway." Gardner walked away to look at some hoof marks. He picked up a broken lariat. He flung it aside and came back. "I'll take a scout for the horses. Get together whatever you want to take with you."

He stood a moment looking at the smoke trailing from the short pipe of the cookstove. "I never saw anything like that." He ground-hitched his packhorse and rode away, in the direction the night raiders had gone.

"I don't like him," Nan said. She was making a pretense of squeezing her injured foot.

Vaughn did not know about Gardner himself; he had been attracted to the man as a casual visitor, but now he did not know whether he liked him or not. "Here, let me at that foot," he said.

He knelt and began to work the bones. Nan's lips twisted in pain. Blood began to seep from the tiny hole in the bottom of her foot, to run down the smooth surface on top where the nail had emerged. "Why didn't you say something before?" Vaughn demanded.

"We had trouble enough."

After a while Gardner returned with Mitch. "The other one is dead. Somebody shot it. It was a good-looking horse. The team—I didn't look for them."

"Corkey was a good Kentucky—"

"They're not built for this country," Gardner said. "Thoroughbreds of any kind don't belong out here." His face was bitter. He looked at a pile of gear that Steele had gathered, some of Nan's clothes, two saddles and a bridle.

He touched a saddle with his foot. "Is that all you're taking, Steele?"

"And this." Vaughn was holding his father's rifle.

"There was a pistol?"

"Somewhere there," Vaughn said. "A Colt."

"Find it."

Vaughn found the pistol.

"Can you shoot one?" Gardner asked.

"Some. I'll learn in time."

The scarred face twisted a little in a mirthless smile. "No doubt—you and that Southern blood of yours."

"There's nothing wrong with my blood, Gardner! We're not asking you for any help."

"Fine, fine." Gardner took a look at the country, at the wrecked homestead. He picked up a saddle and walked toward Mitch. "This beauty doesn't carry double, no doubt?"

"No," Vaughn said.

"Then you can walk, Steele." Gardner saddled up. "If you've got your heart set on town, that's fine for you, Steele, but not for the girl. How old are you, Nan?"

"Twelve."

Gardner cursed under his breath. "Come on. We're going over to the Cloverleaf."

"Hester's place!" Vaughn stared. "He was with the men last night."

"You saw him?"

"No, but—"

"You would have, undoubtedly, if it had been light enough. Come on." Gardner lifted Nan on

Mitch. He put her clothes and the extra saddle on his packhorse. "I suppose you want to carry your rifle, Steele, all by yourself."

Vaughn walked beside Mitch, across the rolling hills, through the slushy snow of the gullies, puzzled and half resentful of the will of this strange man who led toward Cloverleaf. Gardner set a slow pace. He did not look around or inquire of Vaughn how he was getting along.

The Spotted Hills went on forever. Now and then Gardner glanced toward the mountains. Although he did not try to hurry, there seemed to lie in him an urgency; he gave an impression of feeling that he was wasting time. Watching him one time when he glanced toward the Empires and then briefly at Nan, Vaughn saw a fleeting smile, half sardonic, half gentle.

They came in the middle of the afternoon to the lower reaches of Pittsburg Creek, which ran through a wide bottom deep with sod. Lee Hester had been first in the Spotted Hills, and he had made no mistake in picking his spot. There were cattle here, in bunches all along the stream, shorthorns that had wintered well.

Vaughan stopped. "I don't know about this, Gardner. I—"

"I do," Gardner said. "Come on."

They entered a silent yard before a huge log house. To the right, along the hill, there were lesser buildings, a bunkhouse, storerooms, a cookshack. Water carried in the adzed halves of logs ran from an enormous spring made a sparkling fall to a log trough in the yard.

Vaughn had never been here before. He stared around him, half angry, half envious. Two things happened at once. A girl about Vaughn's age came around the shady side of the ranch-house. Her flowered gingham was bright and cool-looking. She wore her hair in pigtails, blonde shining hair that caught the full strike of the sun when she passed the corner of the logs. There was a startled look upon her face.

At the same time a blocky man stepped quickly from one of the storerooms. He was carrying a long strip of rawhide in one hand and a knife in the other. Now he tossed the rawhide behind him and put the knife away. He stared at Gardner. His hand moved toward a pistol on his hip, and then it stopped, and the man's face was no longer surprised but hard and watchful.

"Well, by God!" he said.

It was Anson Dodge, the Cloverleaf foreman. Vaughn had seen him before, riding past the Steele homestead. Once he had stopped, looking long and hard at the two Kentucky horses, grunting when Mrs. Steele had tried to be polite, and then he had ridden across the garden on his way out.

Gardner gave the man no attention.

"Well, by God!" Dodge said, louder this time.

Still Gardner gave him not as much as a glance.

The girl in pigtails said, "Hello there, Mr. Gardner." She looked at Nan, and then her glance flicked quickly over Vaughn. He felt sharp awareness of his dirty clothing, of the heat and tiredness bearing on his body.

Gardner said, "Martha, you're getting uglier ever day." A smile passed with the words and the girl returned the smile.

Martha Hester. Vaughn had heard of her. Her glance brushed him again. The smile that she had held for Gardner died then and she looked away quickly.

"Won't you all come in?" she said.

Gardner swung down. "Just me and Nan, if you please." He introduced the girls, and left Vaughn standing there, leaning on his rifle. Gardner helped Nan from her horse and carried her to the porch.

A tall woman with upswept hair, soft gray, came quickly to the porch with a question in her eyes. "Mr. Gardner, is she hurt?"

"Not bad."

The woman held the door and Gardner went inside, still carrying Nan. The woman gave Vaughn a quick, worried glance and followed. Martha started to say something to Vaughn. She hesitated a moment, and then she too went into the house.

The strangeness of the situation angered Vaughn, but it left him helpless. Partly from his helplessness and partly from odd thoughts about Drake Gardner came the knowledge that he trusted the man.

He walked across the yard and took a tin cup hanging from a peg near the log flume.

"Who said the water was free?" Anson Dodge came up behind him, scowling.

Vaughn drank slowly, watching the man over the cup. The water was so cold it set Vaughan's teeth on edge. This Dodge was a burly, ugly man, although no single feature of his face was misshapen, but everything seemed to be crowded into too little space in the center of his head. His mouth was a meager cut; it might drop with cowardice or be tight with cruelty. His face glistened from recent shaving, and on it lay a darkness of anger.

Gardner had ignored him. Dodge was feeling that. He wanted now, Vaughn sensed, to vent his anger on a weaker man. The devil with Anson Dodge. He was probably one of those who had ridden last night to the shack.

Vaughn hung the cup up and turned away. Dodge caught his shoulder and spun him around. The grip was powerful. The fingers dug and the thumb gouged.

"I asked a question," Dodge said.

"I'll ask one too." Vaughn called the man a foul name. "Where were you last night?"

With his free hand Dodge whacked Vaughn across the mouth. He held him easily and struck again, and then he pushed him into the watering trough, kicking his legs up so that Vaughn was nearly jack-knifed in the deep-cut log. The icy water took his breath away.

Dodge kicked the fallen rifle to one side. He stood there a moment, losing interest in Vaughn, apparently more angered by this small victory than he had been before. His glance swung toward the house.

"Hold a civil tongue, if you ever have the bad sense to come here again, Steele." Still glancing at the house, Dodge started toward the storeroom.

Vaughn scrabbled out of the trough. He picked up the rifle. He knelt and put the front sight in the middle of Dodge's broad back. He cocked the weapon.

"Steele!" Gardner's voice was a whiplash across the yard. "Steele!"

For an instant Vaughn was thrown off, and then he sighted again. The first shot from the porch threw dust against his face. He jerked his head. The rifle went off with a roar. He heard another pistol shot after that, while he was fumbling blindly for another cartridge.

When he could see again, Gardner was walking across the yard, a smoking pistol in his hand. Dodge was lying on the ground, with his knees up, moving them from side·to side, groaning.

CHAPTER 3
Brett

VAUGHN'S FIRST FEELING WAS ONE OF TRIUMPH, AND then he was sick and frightened; he had gut-shot Dodge. Sure as the world, he had put a bullet from the heavy rifle through the man's stomach. He was afraid to go look.

Gardner walked over to the wounded man. He kicked Dodge. "Get up, you scum! You're scratched across the ribs. Get up and get out of my sight."

A cook came out of the mess shack, hesitant about going near the scene. Gardner hauled Dodge to his feet and gave him a vicious shove toward the cook.

"You'll come once too often, Gardner," Dodge said. "You'll come when—"

"Shut up." Gardner put his foot against the man's seat and shoved him violently. The cook came forward and took the foreman by the arm and led him away.

"That was a devil of a thing you tried, Steele." Gardner walked over to Vaughn and stood beside him. "Come on, we're leaving now."

They stopped at the porch. "Martha and you will have to accept my apologies, Mrs. Hester," Gardner said.

The woman looked at him with a pained expression. Years before she must have been a beautiful woman, but now there was something haunted in her look; and yet, behind that, there seemed to be a great capacity for calmness.

The girl, Martha, looked at Vaughn with fear and loathing. "You were going to shoot him in the back!"

"Of course," Gardner said. "Why not?"

The quick reversal bewildered Vaughn.

Nan hopped out on the porch on one leg. "Vaughn! Are you all right?"

"He's all right, Nan," Mrs. Hester said. "You come with me and get your foot back in that pan."

Martha stayed on the porch while Gardner and Vaughn rode away. They went down the creek a half mile and then Gardner cut across the hills, straight toward the mountains.

All at once Vaughn reined in his horse. "That's no place for Nan. I'm going back there and get her."

"It's the only place for her," Gardner said. "It's the only place in the whole miserable country."

"But those Hesters—"

"What about the Hesters?" Gardner stopped

his horse. "Are you talking about the women, or the men?"

"Old Lee, I mean—"

"There's a younger brother there you've never seen. Pray to God that you don't. Are you coming with me or not?"

Vaughn rode on. "Where was Hester?"

"In the house."

"Why didn't he come out?"

"He has a bullet through his shoulder, or maybe it was high in the chest. He wasn't cordial enough to explain."

"From last night?"

Gardner said, "I'd say so. It's a fair guess."

Lee Hester then for sure. Vaughn thought of his feelings last night when he had fallen over his father in the dark. He checked Mitch again. "I'm going back there."

"Go ahead." Gardner did not look back, "Dodge would like it just fine if you went smoking back there by yourself. Try for the front of him this time, Steele."

Gardner's unconcern and the truth of his words threw ice on Vaughn's hot intentions. Once more he went ahead to ride beside the man. "Maybe I shouldn't have tried to shoot him, but I was mad. I didn't care."

"I saw that. There's no particular virtue in shooting a man the hard way. Getting Dodge from the front would be the hard way, too, believe me. There is a code that says murder is all right if done under certain rules. I generally follow it but I don't necessarily subscribe to it, although I do recommend it to those who intend to shoot me."

Gardner spoke carelessly but there was no

jest in his tone or words. Vaughn swung his
horse around on the other side so he would not
have to look at the man's scarred face.

"It's that bad, is it?" Gardner asked. "If it
scares a man who would shoot another in the
back, think what it must do to a woman."

"It wasn't—I didn't—"

"The devil it wasn't my face." Gardner said.
"Now let's forget it, shall we?"

There was no understanding the man at all,
Vaughn thought.

Gardner said, "He spatted you one and you
fell backward into the trough, so that made you
mad enough to try to kill him."

"He held me and pushed me in."

Gardner laughed, curtly, without humor.
"Hot Southern blood and ice water. It should
have cooled you off. You're a prize now. A Rebel's kid who tried to shoot Anson Dodge, after
your father already pinged one through Lee
Hester's shoulder. There's seven ranches in the
Spotted Hills. Your hide would look good on
the stable door of any one of them."

"Don't call my father a Rebel, damn you!"

"Don't tell me anything about the war," Gardner said. "Not one single thing. Make a big fat
note of that. Vaughn Steele, and maybe we'll
get along fine."

The snow-veined mountains seemed to grow
higher as the hills unrolled at their feet. Vaughn
had never been this far west before. He twisted
in the saddle to look at the enormous red carpet
stretching out behind them. Somewhere down
there, lost entirely now, was the hope that had
killed his father.

Vaughn Steele knew that he would never go

back to it. He wished that he had burned what was left of the house, leaving only the long mound to remind him of what he must do someday.

They rode into aspen country. There were no fuzzy blooms upon the branches yet but the trunks of the trees were glistening with new green. Underfoot the leaf mat was thick and damp, spilling in chunks from the feet of the horses.

"Why'd you want to settle way up here?" Vaughn asked.

"Because I did, that's all." Gardner stopped his horse suddenly and swung around. He waved his hand at the country below. "It looks like half the world down there, doesn't it? It's nothing. It's too small now. You're looking at a battlefield, Steele. The lines are already drawn. Didn't any of that ever drift over to you on that homestead?"

"No, I don't know what you're talking about."

"You'll find out." Gardner looked doubtfully at Vaughn. "I can get you out of this country, you and your sister, in a few days. Where would you go?"

There was no place to go. All the loneliness of the world settled down on Vaughn. There was a lump in his chest when he thought of his parents. Here he was, separated from Nan, riding away with a stranger to an unknown destination. In the space of a few days all this had come to him.

"You sure my sister will be all right?"

Gardner spoke with the first gentleness he had shown. "She will. Depend on it."

They came at dusk to a small valley set among the rocks. There was a meadow in the upper part. The long grasses were lying on the ground, combed flat by the recent passing of the snow. A dozen horses, still shaggy from the winter, were grazing in the valley. Where the rocks made an arc at the upper end of the meadow light was showing in the windows of a low cabin.

Gardner dismounted. "Stay here until I call you in." He took his rifle and went ahead on foot.

Sometime later Vaughn saw his shadow pass a window, and then his call came clearly through the growing dark and cold. "All right, Steele."

Vaughn caught up the rope of the packhorse and went on in, too tired now and jarred by the events of the last twenty-four hours to wonder much about Gardner's behavior. A man came out and helped them unpack, not speaking. He was tall and moved with a minimum of effort, and that was all Vaughn could tell about him. Gardner called him Brett.

When they went inside Vaughn saw gear piled against the walls and in the corners, six bunks against the walls, and the general rough set-up of a bachelor house.

Brett's face was youthful, a restless face. Tiny muscles not ordinarily used in normal expressions moved in it when he spoke. When they sat down to eat he took off his hat. His hair was white, thick and straight and shockingly white. Vaughn kept looking at it and at the man's face, not knowing then how old to guess his age.

"What's new around the hills, Drake?" Brett

asked. He seemed to have accepted Vaughn's presence as normal.

"Nothing," Gardner said. "Just building up."

"Uh-huh," Brett said tonelessly. He glanced across the room at Vaughn's pistol and rifle lying on a bunk. "Did you see little Gentle Face this time?"

"Who said I was over there?"

"You were late coming back, that's all."

"My business, Janney. All mine." Gardner looked at Vaughn. "Take the bunk where you left your loot."

Vaughn was drooping in his chair. The heat of the cabin, the long ride, and the drop from tension had loosened everything in him. He stumbled off to bed.

The lamp on the table seemed to burn all night. He half wakened now and then, enough to realize it was still lighted, that the two men were still sitting at the table.

He heard Brett Janney say, "Who is he, Drake?"

"From the shack down there. They wrecked it last night."

"Where does he fit now?"

"Does he have to fit? Does everything have to work out in that cold-blooded mind of yours?"

Janney laughed gently, but it was not a pleasant sound. "I've always said you have a soft spot, Gardner."

"That's my business."

"Up to a point. Then it becomes mine."

"We'll see," Garner said.

Vaughn went back to sleep, into the sweet darkness of rest where nothing could puzzle him, and no guns could speak to him from the night. When he woke up in the morning Brett Janney was gone.

Two men had eaten breakfast, for the tinware was still on the table. There was a fire in the stove and hot coffee in the pot. Vaughn cooked a meal and cleaned up the mess. He walked out into the sunrise, surprised to see that the Spotted Hills were visible through the rift in the rocks where the trail came up.

He walked to the center of the meadow. The shaggy horses edged away from him warily. There was a dark stripe on their backs. They were smaller than Mitch or any of the average run of ranch animals he had seen. There was a wiry tough look about them that said they could winter any place they pleased. He recalled what Gardner had said about thoroughbreds in this country.

The sun swept up the long miles of the Spotted Hills. From here they were beautiful, for this was shelter. Grim and solid sat the mountains and they gave a feeling of security that Vaughn had never felt on the open land.

Drake Gardner came riding from the trees that had root-split granite to hold to life around the edges of the meadow. He was a slouching rider, sitting his horse as if it were merely an extension of his own body. For the first time Vaughn saw the man's face as a whole, without the scarred side standing out alone. In a way, it was not nearly as startling as Janney's mobile features thrown in sharp contrast against his snow-white hair.

Impulsively, and not from raw curiosity,

Vaughn asked, touching his own cheek, "How'd you get that?"

"A fool threw a bucket of water on the breech of a red-hot cannon while we were waiting for the battery to cool. I was the luckiest one of the whole crew."

Gardner stared at the hills. "Pretty, huh?"

"I like it better right here. There's something you can put your back against."

"Oh?" Gardner gave the youth an odd look. "Yeah. Living down there on the flats. I see. But you better learn, Steele, that you can't put your back against anything, because there is never anything but yourself behind you. You're sure you don't want to leave the Spotted Hills for good?"

"Not this part of it."

"Why?"

"Someone killed my father. I—"

"Someone killed my father too, and my mother, and my two brothers. I'd be a damned fool if I spent my life trying to get even over that. There were ten men, at least, in that mob at your shack, Steele. No one will ever know who shot your father. You'd better forget about it."

"Forget about it!" Vaughn cursed. "They might have killed my sister too. They didn't care!"

"Lee Hester wouldn't have been there if he'd known Nan was home. I'll bet he thought she was still in town. He wouldn't have let any of his men—"

"You're pretty thick with the Hesters, Gardner."

"I hate Lee, and I hate his brother, Finlay, even worse."

"You go right to their place and—"

"Shoot their foreman. That was your fault, Steele."

"*You* shot Dodge? I thought—"

"You thought you nicked him with that rifle. I know. I knocked dirt in your eyes with one shot and raked another across his ribs just when he was leveling down on you, Steele. Your shot put a hole in the rooster's tail on the wind-vane, I think—on top of the barn."

CHAPTER 4
Men Shoot Back

VAUGHN BLINKED. HE OWED THIS MAN A LOT. FIRST, for seeing that Nan was taken care of; and then for several other things. If he could not understand some of Gardner's actions, he still was bound by loyalty to him.

With a wondering sort of bitterness, Gardner sat looking down at him. "Get that pistol, Steele. Let's see what you can miss with it."

The separater from a case of crackers was big at twenty paces. Vaughn's grip was natural and loose; his eyes were good and his nerves were young and steady. He slammed his shots fairly close to the middle of the target.

"Try again," Gardner said.

Vaughn let off one more careful shot after reloading. He was aiming when the pistol blasted, almost against him, it seemed. He felt the gush of heat across one ear, the sting of powder grains. His shot went someplace and he had no idea where.

Gardner put his own pistol away, his eyes inscrutable. "Got the idea? Men like to shoot back."

In the days to come Vaughn learned to shoot a pistol at a target, not flinching when Gardner fired beside him, no jerking when Gardner yelled wildly, trying to hold steady even when Gardner shoved him.

"I don't know," Gardner said. "You might become too good at it. You might get the idea that calling out a man and facing him like a gentleman is honorable and good. Someday you might decide it was time to shoot Anson Dodge from the front. Then I could bury you."

"What makes Dodge so tough?"

"Cowardice, and ambition. He also would like—" Gardner stopped suddenly and walked away from the target area near the rocks. "I'll go with you some day to see Nan. Don't ever try it alone."

A rider from Cloverleaf had been to the valley the week before, to carry a message saying that Nan's foot was all right. The courier had been uneasy. He watched the rocks around Gardner's place; he stared at Gardner himself in fear; and he left soon after the message was delivered.

That night across a hot lamp in the low-roofed cabin Vaughn studied Gardner. He liked the man now; he trusted him. He had come to think the thing that Brett Janney had spoken, that Gardner had a large soft spot in him, not weakness, but inherent decency that the man tried to hide with curtness.

"How come you could take Nan right to Clo-verleaf and be sure she would be welcome—after what the Hesters did to us?"

Gardner frowned. "The Hesters don't, not even Finlay, take their brutalness out on women, at least not by violence."

"I've never seen Finlay."

"That's too bad." Gardner rose and started to undress.

"I want to go see my sister."

"Tomorrow."

Vaughn undressed and got into his bunk. "Who are all these extra bunks for?"

"Anyone that needs a bed."

"No one comes here."

"Not since you've been around, just Janney."

"Who's he?"

"An old acquaintance."

After a while Vaughn said, "You don't ever sell any of those horses you breed."

"The strain is not right yet. Shut up, Steele."

In the dead of night Vaughn heard the hail. He grabbed his pistol and swung out of bed and padded barefoot to the door. There he collided in the darkness with Gardner.

"It's all right," Gardner said. "Light the lamp." He opened the door and called, "All right, Janney."

There were five of them. White-haired Brett Janney was the only one Vaughn had seen be-fore. They came in like they lived here. A flat-nosed man with a curling black beard tasted the water, then tossed the dipperful on the floor. He looked at Vaughn. "Get a fresh bucket, kid."

Vaughn said, "Get it yourself, or ask in an-other tone."

Janney laughed. "He learns fast from you, Drake." He looked at the bearded man. "Go get your water, Sloss. You know where the creek runs."

Gardner sat at the table, smoking his pipe in measured puffs. He watched the men cook a meal and wolf it down. Except for Janney, they ate as if they had not seen food for a long time. Janney's hands were long and slender. He cut his bacon up in small pieces. He wiped his lips afterward, looking with delicate distaste at the soiled bandanna he used.

There was little speech, but enough for Vaughn to realize that four of the men spoke with the slurred accent of the South. Sloss' lips were thin and red in his beard. He watched Vaughn thoughtfully at times.

The meal over, Janney took a cheroot from his pocket. "It's growing a little tiresome on the other side."

"Maybe you'll get used to it," Gardner said.

"I'm afraid not. The men don't like it either."

"Not a bit," Sloss said. "Not one bit."

Vaughn looked from face to face. They were watching Gardner, and the tension was full and thick.

Janney said, "You haven't changed your mind, have you, Drake?"

"I never made it up in the first place."

"Ah, yes. I began to suspect that when I was here last. That's why we came again so soon."

"No," Gardner said. "Not your way, Janney."

"What's your way?"

"There isn't any."

Janney smiled. "Let's not say that. Charley Burgett and Troutt Warner don't think so." He yawned, but there was tension even in that. He looked around at the four who had come with him. "Suppose we talk about it again in the morning, Drake; just you and I, without the doubtful benefit of these hairy, drooping ears."

"We can talk," Gardner said. "No difference though."

"There might be," Janney said. "There always has been where—"

"That's enough." Gardner had put on his pants and boots, and he had thrust his pistol into the waistband of his pants. The lamplight gave his face an evil, waiting look, heightening, rather than softening, the pits and scars on the one side.

Vaughn saw a careful weighing, mixed with fear, in the eyes of four men who watched Gardner; but he saw only a deadly sort of amusement on Janney's face. The muscles of Janney's cheeks and forehead rippled easily when he smiled. For an instant Vaughn wondered if the man could flick a certain area of his skin to scare a fly away. It gave him a queasy feeling to think about it.

Gardner's live dark eyes caught sharp points of light and jetted them. He was sitting sidewise at the table, with one leg braced solidly against it. Sloss shifted his arms casually, placing both hands against the edge of the table on his side.

Gardner's eyes touched Sloss like the tip of a whip. "You wouldn't try to jam me in against

the wall, would you, Max? You might need both
those hands to hold your guts in if you tried."

"Max was never very subtle," Janney said. He
yawned again. "Get up and go to bed, you ox!"

The bearded man came up from the table
slowly. His teeth gleamed white as he tried to
pass it off with a twisted smile. He walked down
the narrow room, sat on Vaughn's bunk, and
started to remove his boots.

"That's my bed," Vaughn said.

"It was." Sloss grunted as he tugged at his
boots. "You can have it back tomorrow."

Both Gardner and Janney were watching
Vaughn. What lay on Gardner's face the youth
could not tell, but the fixed, waiting set of the
man seemed to demand decision.

"Get off my bed."

"You've got a big mouth, son. You've been too
long around Gardner."

Vaughn glanced once more from the corner
of his eye at Gardner, and then he kicked with
his heavy shoe as hard as he could. The toe
caught Sloss full in the beard. It straightened
him up from bending toward his boots. His
head rapped hard against the bunk above him.

Wide-eyed, he sat there loosely. Vaughn
grabbed him by the shirt front and hauled him
up, intending to push him toward the end of the
room. The man came to life with a grunt. He
knocked Vaughn across the room. Sloss shook
his head and started after Vaughn.

Once more Vaughn glanced at Gardner. Both
he and Janney were still seated, watching but
apparently unconcerned.

Sloss hurled himself across the room. Vaughn
slid along the wall. The bearded man crashed

hard against the logs, bringing down a fine sprinkle of dirt from the roof.

Janney murmured, "I said he wasn't subtle."

Sloss turned, kicking at a saddle that lay across his feet. His eyes were dazed. He hunched his shoulders and started toward Vaughn again. Vaughn raised on his toes and with all his might brought down the stick of aspen wood he had snatched from a pile beside the stove.

It made a sodden sound on Sloss' head. Vaughn struck again while the man was groping toward him. Sloss fell to his knees, shaking his head. He began to rise slowly. Vaughn reached to the wall beside his bunk and got his pistol. He started to use it as a club, and then he cocked it.

"Never mind!" Gardner said sharply.

"Your bed, I'd say." Janney laughed. "Wouldn't you, Max?"

Sloss lurched past Vaughn and sat down on a bunk against the end wall. He twisted his head from side to side, holding one hand spread on the top of his skull.

Janney's other companions moved quietly, preparing to turn in. One of them, a squat man with a bald head spotted with great freckles, looked across the room and winked solemnly at Vaughn.

"This mountain air does things to a man, Drake," Janney said. The little dips and trenches moved with his smile, but his eyes were bleakly speculative as he looked at Vaughn.

Gardner and Vaughn talked inside after

breakfast, telling the others to go see that the sun came up all right.

Vaughn went to the meadow. Green was rising among the dead grasses of long summer. Vaughn called Mitch, and the animal tossed gouts of earth and wisps of grass from flying hooves as it galloped to him. Gardner's horses caught the smell of the morning, snorting and kicking as they raced down the meadow.

The world was young, Vaughn thought; and this had been a wonderful place before Janney and Sloss came.

The bald man who had winked at Vaughn left his three companions at the small corral and came out to Vaughn. "Fair piece of horseflesh there," he said loudly. Frog was this man's name. His mouth was wide and puckered and if he had any teeth at all they were not in front.

He walked around Mitch. From the side away from Vaughn he said in an almost inaudible voice, "Don't ever let Max get his hands on you, kid. You would have been ahead last night if you'd pulled that trigger."

"Who are you fellows?"

Frog patted Mitch's shoulder. "Would you sell him?" His voice was normal again.

"Where do you come from, Frog?"

The man glanced toward the mountains. "Well, maybe I don't blame you for not wanting to sell him." He walked back to the corral, where his companions were watching.

Vaughn was chopping wood when Gardner and Janney came out. Janney was not smiling now. There was a cold tightness in Gardner's manner.

Janney said, "Saddle up."

Before the five rode toward the Spotted Hills, Max Sloss licked his red lips and shook his head at Vaughn. Gardner watched until the long folds of the land took the riders. The grass was coming down there now, irregular patches of it against the red, making the pattern that gave the hills their name.

Gardner's face was grim. "Did you enjoy that show you put on last night, Steele?"

"No."

"You wanted to show me you could take care of yourself, huh? How far would you have gone without me around?"

"It was my bunk."

"My bunk," Gardner said. "My land. My slaves. My right, no matter what." He started toward the house. "We'll go to Cloverleaf now."

"What does Janney and those others do?"

Gardner went inside without answering. To hell with him then, Vaughn thought. He did not ask any more questions during the morning's ride.

On the creek below Cloverleaf they met Lee Hester riding a long-legged bay. One of his arms was in a black sateen sling. He nodded to Gardner and some inner amusement twisted his face.

"You stayed away longer than usual, Drake." Mockery came with the words, puzzling Vaughn and irritating him. No one seemed to care if he knew what was going on. He kept staring at Hester, trying to feel deep anger against the man, this handsome, arrogant man who had come by dark to the Steel homestead to wreck and murder.

It came as a surprise to Vaughn that his feelings did not touch the peak he thought they should. He hated Lee Hester and always would, but he did not want to kill him.

Gardner was watching Vaughn narrowly; and it was because of that steady scrutiny that Hester turned his eyes. He said. "I did not know your sister was in the house that night, Steele. For your further information, my men were all unarmed."

Vaughn said nothing.

"Your white-haired friend has ridden to the Wagonwheel, Hester," Gardner said.

"A waste of time. Burgett and Warner are my friends."

"Ask Finlay about that. He draws more truth about men from the air than you ever could by studying them."

Hester smiled thinly. "Brother Protector, why don't you move to Cloverleaf? Or could you stand that?" He watched Gardner's face turn white, ashen on one side, hideously splotched against the scars on the other. "No, Drake, I don't believe you could." Hester laughed and rode away, "Excuse me. Spring roundup."

Nan and Martha Hester were working in a flower garden beside the house when Gardner and Vaughn rode in. Nan dropped a spade and came running to Vaughn. Her face was radiant. Whatever blight of uncertainty lay on Cloverleaf, it had not touched her, Vaughn thought.

"Where have you been so long, Vaughn?"

Vaughn nodded toward the mountains. He was glad to see this girl who threw her arms around him, but he was embarrassed by the act. Martha Hester stood at the edge of the garden, watching. Her hair was up today, and the effect gave her a startling resemblance to her mother, without the strained, haunted look of Mrs. Hester.

"I've got a room all by myself!" Nan said. "You'll have to see it. Martha and I— You never talked to Martha when you were here before, did you?" Nan pulled him toward the girl. "This is my brother, Martha."

Martha smiled and spoke as if she had not known the fact before. Vaughn dragged his hat off, conscious that his hair was overlong and probably disordered. The heavy pistol on his hip seemed out of place. He bowed without thinking, a gesture that his father had taught him long ago; and now it seemed betrayal of Carmody Steele to be acting so at the Hester Place.

Gardner had already gone into the house. Suddenly awkward in his heavy shoes, Vaughn stumbled back and picked up the reins of the horses. "I'd better give them a drink."

Nan chattered at his side while he let the horses drink. He looked uneasily at the house and at the other silent buildings.

"Mr. Hester's brother, Finlay, is nice," Nan said. "He sent a man out to put a board on father's grave."

"He did?" Vaughn had thought of doing so himself. *Pray that you don't meet Finlay ...* Gardner said. Now Nan said he was nice. Confused and troubled, Vaughn stared at the house. Martha went up the steps. "I'll start straightening up your room, Nan, so you can show it to your brother."

Mrs. Hester came to the porch. "Put the horses in the corral, if you wish, Mr. Steele. You and Mr. Gardner will have dinner with us."

"They really do eat here, Vaughn," Nan said.

"Yeah? Are you ashamed of the way we used to live?"

"No, but— There's something funny about you, Vaughn. You act a lot older than you used to. It's only been a few weeks, but you're changed."

Inside, the house seemed larger than it did from outside. Two hallways ran from a large livingroom toward winged L's on each side of the central area. Gardner was pacing the livingroom. He barely glanced at Vaughn when Nan rushed him down one of the halls to see her room. It was large and comfortable, and there were furnishings in it that had never been in the Steele shack.

"Mother used to talk about things like this," Nan said. "Isn't it wonderful?"

Vaughn was vaguely dissatisfied, suspicious of what seemed like finery to him. Somewhere in his background there had been finer rooms than this, but all that meant nothing to him now, for he had heard only his parents' talk before the war.

Mrs. Hester was talking to Gardner when Vaughn returned to the livingroom. There was a haunted bleakness on his face too, it seemed to Vaughn. Damn, but this was an odd place.

CHAPTER 5
Gentle Face

THE DINNER DID NOT CHANGE ANYTHING. VAUGHN observed that Gardner barely ate. The rest of the time he kept watching Mrs. Hester, his black eyes lifting to her as if he were looking against his will, or without conscious knowledge of the act.

They finished in silence. Mrs. Hester said, "Perhaps Mr. Steele would like to see your father's horses, Martha."

"He probably would," Martha said. "Uncle Finlay wants to see him first, though."

"Oh?" Mrs. Hester gave Gardner a startled look.

"Why not, Molly?" Gardner shrugged.

"I'll show him," Nan said. Going down the hall with Vaughn, she whispered, "Uncle Finlay is awful nice, Vaughn. It's too bad about him."

She knocked on a door and a soft voice said,

"Yes, Nan, tell your brother to come in, and would you please look once more for the violets there in the damp by the spring. They should be out by now."

The room was furnished in dark oak. A shade halfway down on an enormous window let slanting light rest in a bright wall on the feet and legs of a gentle-looking man who sat in a straight-backed chair near a bed. There was a tray of food on a table beside him.

"You would be young Vaughn Steele?"

"Yes."

"Stand right there a moment and say that again, please."

Utterly puzzled, Vaughn obeyed. Finlay Hester tilted his head, nodding. His face had the pink look of baby skin. His hair was jet black, and his eyes held a patient, seeking look.

"About six feet. Large for your age," he said. "Now walk over to that armchair—don't tiptoe, please—and sit down."

Once more Vaughn obeyed. He was still halfway across the room from Hester, who sat in his own uncomfortable chair with what seemed to Vaughn to be back-breaking stiffness.

"You must weigh a hundred and seventy-five pounds, Mr. Steele."

"I guess so."

"And you fully intended to shoot Anson Dodge sometime ago. Did you leave a pistol outside when you came here today?"

"Yes, sir."

"Are you proficient with it? Oh, never mind." Hester wiped out the question with a wave of his hand. "You would be, of course, being with

Drake Gardner any length of time at all. How do you like Drake?"

The man had cocked his head to the other side now. He had the softest voice, the most gentle manner Vaughn had ever known. *Gentle Face!* That was the name Brett Janney had used. *Did you see little Gentle Face this time?*

"How do you like Drake, Mr. Steele?"

"Fine."

"Of course. And Janney?"

"I don't like him."

"How many men did Brett have with him the last time he came?"

"Four."

"They went back over the mountains, as usual, I suppose?"

"They went to Wagonwheel."

There was a pause as sharp as a flung question. "I see," Hester said. "I would say that you did not care for any of those men." He waited. "Your silence is sufficient. Another important consideration: How do you feel about the death of your father? I mean, about the men who killed them."

"I hate them."

"That is natural. You don't realize it, of course, but your father persisted in bringing about his fate. He belonged to a lost group. He was further lost when your mother recognized basic facts that he refused to see. She acted. He clung to nothing. Your sister is a charming youngster, Mr. Steele. I assume she is greatly like her mother."

"No," Vaughn said. "She's like my father."

"That can be corrected. I've wandered a little, Mr. Steele. Let us move toward a more immediate point. When you started to kill Anson Dodge, was it utter rage that made you act as you did, or were you impelled by the more logical view that the task could be best accomplished without the dragging impediments of code and honor. I refer, of course, to your attempted method."

"You mean was I out of my head, or did I figure I ought to kill him anyway I could get him?"

"Roughly put, but correct. How was it?"

"I don't know."

"Ah! That is encouraging. We have had too much prattle of honor around here for too long." Hester cleared his throat. ."Step over there to the window, please. Don't bother to raise the shade. Merely pull it back a little and tell me what you see."

Vaughn did as he was directed. Against the hill was a lattice house covered with vines that were just beginning to unfold their leaves. Drake Gardner was standing there, looking down at Mrs. Hester. She shook her head.

Vaughn Steele's experience was limited, but he had seen his father look at his mother with that same intense, tender expression. He let the shade swing back against the window casing. The one short look had given him a view of a Drake Gardner he did not know at all. He went quickly across the room and sat down.

Finlay Hester had taken the tray from the table beside him. He was eating, lifting his food with over-careful movements, almost dainty in his preciseness. Vaughn was reminded then of Brett Janney. Suddenly an uneasy feeling began to mount toward fear. There was something

strange and evil here, something akin to the
crawling sensation that Vaughn had felt when
he wondered if Janney could jerk any given por-
tion of his flesh, like an animal.

"You saw. I suppose it must have startled
you, Mr. Steele."

Vaughn was not Mr. Steele; he was a boy who
wanted to get out of this room, into the clean
sunlight. But he sat where he was, repelled and
fascinated by the erect figure in the straight-
backed chair.

"They have loved each other a long time,"
Hester said. "A man not hampered by code and
honor would have taken her from my brother,
who did not deserve her in the first place. But
not the gallant Drake. Oh no! He merely sits in
his eyrie there in the mountains, a slave to puny
man-made law."

Hester put his fork down as if the food had
lost taste. He set the tray on the table, lifting it
high and letting it down quite gently. "I had
hopes for Drake Gardner, my boy, but the war
brought out a latent defect in him, the stupidity
called honor.

"Now you are different. You have made a
good start, although I would have been tempo-
rarily embarrassed by the loss of Anson Dodge.
You can serve where Gardner failed. There is
one man who is a festering sore in the Spotted
Hills. When he is gone things will arrange
themselves, with some direction, of course.

"I mean Brett Janney. Kill him for me, Mr.
Steele, and you will be rewarded well."

"Kill him!"

"Why, yes. By any means you see fit, as ex-
pediently as you would have shot Anson Dodge.

Once that is done, return to me here. Believe me, the world will begin to unfold for you in its true perspective then. You will begin to understand that kings are made, not born. As a small start to aid your present limited understanding—" Hester opened a drawer in the table at his elbow and pulled out a small packet. The rectangle of sunlight reached from his polished boots to slender, pale hands that held the packet.

"As a meager start, but important in its way, here is five hundred dollars." Hester flipped the packet across the room. It struck Vaughn's chest and dropped to his lap.

All at once his fear was overwhelming terror. Hester's head was cocked to one side, and his seeking eyes looked at Vaughn with fixed attention. The man was smiling gently. Vaughn stumbled to his feet. He put the money on the chair and started to run from the room.

"Come now." Hester frowned. "Have I made a mistake? Surely I haven't, have I?"

Looking back at Hester, Vaughn flung the door open, keeping his hand on the knob. He jerked when someone touched his arm. Nan was standing in the hall with a tiny bunch of woods violets in her hand. She put her finger on her lips, shaking her head to indicate silence. Stupidly, Vaughn stared at her.

"I did make a slight misjudgment, I see," Hester said. "Fear, I suppose, instead of honor, was the deterrent this time. Ah, well . . ." Hester sighed. "If you see Nan before you leave, please tell her I am waiting for the violets."

She was standing there in full view of him.

Vaughn knew then that Finlay Hester was blind.

"I'm here Uncle Finlay!" Nan cried. "And I've got something too!"

Vaughn watched her dart into the room. She gave the tiny bouquet to Hester. He raised it to his face and his smile was beatific as he inhaled the scent; and all the time the blind eyes seemed to be looking straight at Vaughn.

"Your brother and I just had a most interesting chat, Nan."

Vaughn went quickly down the hall. He startled Mrs. Hester, who was looking from a livingroom window. Outside, Drake Gardner was leading his and Vaughn's horses from the corral.

"I think Mr. Gardner is ready to leave." A bleak, drained expression on Mrs. Hester's face did not change. "Come see us again soon, Mr. Steele. Nan misses you a great deal."

Just before Vaughn mounted Nan raced down the steps and embarrassed him again by hugging him while Martha watched from the porch with an amused smile. Nan said, "Wasn't Uncle Finlay the nicest man you ever met?"

Vaughn glanced at Gardner.

"She'll be all right," Gardner said. "Don't worry."

They rode down the creek. Gardner was silent, brooding.

Vaughn said, "That Finlay—"

"I know. He puts a chill on a man. God knows why kids and women think he's fine."

They passed a herd of cattle being held by three men. Anson Dodge was on the ground, tightening his cinch. The hostility of his glance and poise came across fifty yards of space like a shout.

"Finlay Hester's eyes," Gardner said. "Lately they have been corrupted, but Finlay doesn't know it."

There was a black mood on Gardner. When they came to the place where they should have turned to return to the mountains, he rode straight ahead.

"Where are we going?" Vaughn asked.

"To town!" Gardner was savage.

He was in love with Mrs. Hester and he could not do anything about it. Vaughn tried to think of what a man should do in a case like that. He did not know. He recalled how his father had come apart after Faith Steele left. Maybe there was good reason for Gardner's mood.

"Nan said he put a headboard on my father's grave."

"Finlay? Sure. He loves to advertise a dead Rebel. Who do you think sent those men out that night, Steele?"

"Him?"

"Yes, him! Cloverleaf is his, not Lee's."

It came to Vaughn how little he knew of anything in the Spotted Hills; how close his bondage to the soil of Elk Run had been. "He offered me five hundred dollars to kill Brett Janney. Why did he pick me? I'm just—"

"You earned it by the way you acted the first time we went to Cloverleaf. He picked you because Anson Dodge isn't man enough, and because I won't kill Janney without an excuse—and maybe not even with an excuse."

"I don't know what's going on! I don't—"

"Maybe it's a good thing," Gardner said. "For

a brat fresh off a homestead you've done plenty lately. You've attracted Finlay Hester's attention, and you've marked yourself with Janney's gang. You don't seem to have to know what's going on to get into trouble."

Vaughn said surlily, "I don't have to go to town with you, or anywhere else."

"No, you can go back to Cloverleaf and take that five hundred. Finlay's probably laughing now because you didn't take his blood money and walk out with it, without any intention of earning it. That's what he would have done."

"I don't want money made that way."

Gardner grunted.

"Is Lee Hester like Finlay?"

"No. He's the next thing to helplessness there ever was behind a handsome face. He's as dumb about what's going on as you are."

"He's dumb, huh? He wasn't so dumb but what he got the woman you wanted."

Gardner's face turned gray. He shot a wicked look at Vaughn and for a moment Vaughn thought he was going to curse violently.

"Who told you that?" Gardner asked.

"I looked out of the window of Finlay's room. For a dumb brat fresh off a homestead, I still know one or two things when I see them."

"Finlay told you to look!" Gardner cursed Finlay Hester then. He would not talk any more on the ride to town.

Gettysburg clung hard against the railroad, board shacks that drew their sustenance from iron instead of soil. The town was weathered, dirty; it did not have the appeal to Vaughn that it once had offered. When they stabled their horses at Burnett's livery, the train from the east was whistling in the distance.

Gardner said, "That conductor doesn't make this run any more, in case you're looking for trouble."

"What makes you say I always look for trouble?"

"Maybe you don't." Gardner's tone was different then. Vaughn realized that the man's curtness from the very first might have been partly from an effort to make him and Nan forget their grief and shock over Carmody Steele's death.

"I'll be here a while," Gardner said. He held two ten dollar notes toward Vaughn. "Those clodhoppers you're wearing look like hell. So do your pants and shirt. What do you think Nan and Martha must have thought of them?"

"I'll pay you back."

"Pay! Pay! Everybody tries to pay something in this world, even Finlay Hester. He was standing right beside me when that gun blew up. He's been trying to pay somebody for it ever since."

Vaughn made what he thought was a shrewd guess. "Was it Brett Janney who threw the bucket of water on the cannon?"

"Oh hell! The man who did that got the breech of the piece right through his stomach. Brett Janney was—" Gardner looked sourly at Vaughn. "I'll see you." He strode down the street.

CHAPTER 6
"You're Just a Kid!"

VAUGHN BOUGHT NEW CLOTHES. HE WENT TO A BAR-
ber shop for a haircut and bath. Sitting in the
chair while the barber clipped and sheared, he
watched Charley Burgett of the Wagonwheel
pull up with a spring wagon across the street,
in front of the general store.

"I hear you're up there with Drake Gardner
now," the barber said.

"Yeah."

After a while the barber asked, "Hear anything of your ma?"

"No."

The barber eased away to more comfortable
ground. "Those five men of Burgett and Warner's at Wagonwheel sure must be eaters. Now
that's the second time this week Charley's been
in town loading up with grub."

"Five men?"

"The regular crew. They must eat enough for a dozen men, I'd say."

Brett Janney's bunch had gone to Wagon- wheel, Gardner had said. They must be staying there. What then did that mean? All the shreds of half statements and his own guesses swirled in Vaughn's mind, but they would not coalesce.

"How does Lee Hester and Wagonwheel get along?" Vaughn asked.

"Well," the barber said cautiously, "there's some feeling there, I hear." He watched Charley Burgett and a clerk lift a barrel of flour into the wagon. "Charley's a good customer of mine. There's some feeling between the two ranches, I hear." He glanced at Vaughn's pistol belt hanging on an elkhorn rack in the corner.

"What does Drake Gardner think about the situation, Steele?"

"I don't know."

"He's pretty thick with the Hesters."

"Is he?"

"I hear that," the barber said quickly. "You know, a person can hear most anything."

The barber watched Vaughn from the sides of his eyes while the youth strapped on his pis- tol belt. "Going home tonight?"

"Next week."

Vaughn stood on the street a moment. There had been a chance to find out a great deal of gossip, but he had become disgusted and cut the barber off short. It was too much like peer- ing from the window at Gardner and Mrs. Hes- ter. Still, there were many things he would like to know.

He walked across the street. Burgett was tying a tarpaulin over his supplies. He was a tall man with sloping shoulders and heavy wrists that ran far beyond the cuffs of his linsey shirt. His eyes were deepset beside blistered cheekbones. He wore a pistol in his waistband. There was rust upon the hammer, and it looked as if the rust might extend on down to seal the hammer into the frame.

"Lots of visitors at your place, Burgett?"

"What makes you ask?"

"I wondered."

"Uh-huh." Burgett rubbed red stubble on his cheeks. "Been around the homestead lately, Steele?"

"The last time was several weeks ago, at night."

Burgett nodded. His gaze kept wandering up and down the street. He did not know exactly where Gardner was.

"Were you there that night, Burgett?"

The rancher stared. The sharp directness of the question laid guilt across his eyes.

"There's lots of hills out there, Burgett. They dip and rise and there's rocks and trees. If I were you I'd clean the rust off that pistol."

"By God, you've tried to put on weight since you took up with Drake Gardner!"

Vaughn said, "I never had reason to before. Look behind every hill you come to from now on, Burgett."

"You're just a kid!" Some of that was surprise and much of it was fear and wondering.

Vaughn Steele learned quickly wherein the marks of cowardice lie. Burgett was afraid of him. It gave Vaughn a heady feeling. Let the man ride forever with the fear that a bullet would seek him out from ambush someday. He had fired in the night at rifle flashes near a lurching shack. Let the memory of that and the words Vaughn had spoken feed the worms of fear in his brain from now on.

Vaughn learned much; but he learned too little. He turned and started down the street. Instants later he heard Drake Gardner say, "No, Burgett, no."

Gardner was standing in the doorway of the store, his pistol in his hand. Burgett's pistol was half drawn, and he was looking at Vaughn, and his face was twisted.

"Go home, Charley," Gardner said. "Tell Janney and Warner anything that comes to mind."

After Burgett drove away, Gardner walked down to Vaughn. He gave the youth a savage look. "You see what it feels like, what you started to do to Dodge?"

"I was bluffing him. I didn't think he—"

"You wear a pistol. You lack ten years of experience in knowing how to use it. Go to Mrs. Trotter's boarding house, Steele, and go to bed. I'll come there after you when it's time to go home."

Vaughn said, "Yes, sir."

Mrs. Trotter hugged him. She smelled of cooking grease and sweat. "I've been worried sick about you and Nan. I can't understand how she ever went to the Hesters."

"The women there are all right."

"By hell, how could they be! Look what them Hesters done to your pa, boy."

Before he finished eating, Vaughn learned another thing: Gardner had been right, a railroad

boarding house was no place to raise a girl. But
neither could he leave Nan at Cloverleaf forever; he did not know what to do.

The room Vaughn went to held an odor like a
day coach after two nights of being crowded
with passengers. A dusty heat came in with the
night wind from the railroad yards, and then
the framing members of the building began to
creak when late coolness spread from the hills.
Vaughn tossed on a lumpy mattress, thinking
of his bunk at Gardner's place, thinking of the
cool wind brushing curtains in the dainty room
where Nan slept at Cloverleaf.

He wondered what Martha's room was like,
and he wondered if she would notice his new
clothes the next time he rode to Cloverleaf. Finlay Hester's gentle face and the press of evil in
the darkened room where he had sat were all
mixed up with the blotched, murderous expression on Charley Burgett's face when he would
have shot Vaughn in the back.

Rest had barely come to Vaughn when Mrs.
Trotter shook him, standing by his bed with a
brass lamp in her hand, in a shapeless sleeping
dress, with her hair all wild about her face.

"Get Drake Gardner out of town," she said.
"Did you tell anyone you were going to stay
here a week?"

Vaughn could not remember; and anyway the
question seemed to have no point. He swung out
of bed, groping for his pants.

"There's talk. By daylight men from Wagonwheel are coming here for Drake. It might be
later but that makes no difference. Get Drake
and go home. He's in the back room of the Spot-

ted Hills saloon. Now get to hell moving, Vaughn."

The town lay dead. There was no light in the Spotted Hills saloon. Vaughn shivered in the pre-dawn cold. A friendly dog came out from a bed in a pile of manure and huddled against his legs, thumping the ground with its tail.

"She said the back room," Vaughn muttered, and the dog took the words as approval and thumped the ground more violently. Vaughn went to the livery stable. A sleepy hostler cursed and said, "Two dollars, and get them yourself, at this hour. You people never come or go at a decent time."

Vaughn paid. A dirty lantern made a cavern of the stable as he went along the stalls. He passed the rump of a sorrel horse, and then he turned and went back, moving in an empty stall beside it, holding the lantern high. The sorrel was warm. It rattled its halter when it swung its head at him nervously; and then he recognized the blaze mark.

Brett Janney's horse.

Vaughn ran back to the stairway and called, "When did that sorrel come in?"

"Just before I went to sleep the last time, fifteen minutes ago."

"There's two more dollars here under the lantern. Saddle mine and Gardner's and bring them to the Spotted Hills saloon right away."

He heard the hostler sigh. The man's bare feet came down with a thump on the loft floor. "I guess I was never meant to sleep."

The dog leaped beside Vaughn's knee as he ran down the street. He went behind a row of buildings, stumbling over cans and broken bottles. And then he slowed to a walk and felt his way to where a dim light showed at the back of the Spotted Hills. There was a grayish scum upon the glass and the corners of the window were rounded with spider webs.

Gardner was sitting at a table under a Rivers lamp. Brett Janney sat across from him, his hat pushed back on his white hair. There was a whiskey bottle and one glass upon the table. The scarred side of Gardner's face was toward Vaughn. He saw the sweat on it.

"—The difference you asked about—I can trust you if you give your word, Drake," Janney said. "I can't trust Burgett and Warner and Anson Dodge. I have their word and they have mine—"

"And neither is any good," Gardner said. He poured a drink and took it slowly.

"That's right." The creases ran on Janney's face.

"I told you how it was yesterday."

"I don't believe you. You'll get everything you want out of it. How can you turn it down?"

"I am."

"He stole her, Drake. Lee knew you weren't dead. He talked to a man who saw you in the hospital. He let her believe the report and stole her."

"Damn you! Leave her out of this!"

"I can't. She's all you want, Drake."

"I'm not in it!"

"You are. It was in your mind when you came here. That's why you built those extra bunks in your cabin, and told us to drop in anytime. Even

dumb Max Sloss caught on. Who are you trying
to fool, Drake? Take another drink."

Gardner drank automatically. He shook his
head at Janney. "No." There was no force in the
refusal.

"If I thought you'd take her and leave, I
wouldn't worry, but I know you won't. You're
against us, Drake, if you're not with us. I'll have
enough to handle all the rest, without that. You
planned it. You planned it from the first."

Gardner put both hands on his forehead. His
elbow knocked over the glass. It rolled in an arc
toward the edge of the table. Janney waited until it fell. He caught it, refilled it, and set it before Gardner.

"You had it in mind to drive Lee into the
ground and take Molly," Janney said. "What's
wrong about that?"

"I changed my mind," Gardner mumbled.

The admission startled Vaughn but his loyalty to Gardner was not affected. The sight of
Janney, smiling, twisting the barbs of his words
into a helpless man brought a fearful rage.
Vaughn drew his pistol and aimed at Janney's
chest. Things that Gardner had flung at him
stopped him. He let the pistol drop to arm's
length at his side. It struck the dog and brought
a tiny yelp. "Here, Sport!" Vaughn whispered
frantically. The dog leaned into his legs, brushing the ground with its tail.

"I made a long ride," Janney said. "The others are coming, but they won't stop to talk, not
after that deal the kid forced you into today.
Tell me I'm right about you, Drake, and I can
handle Warner and the rest."

"You're wrong. Get out of here!"

The loose motion of Janney's smiling face was far worse than Gardner's scars. Janney shook his head gently. In that moment he was everything to Vaughn that Finlay Hester was. Janney rose, stepping back. "I taunted you about that soft spot, not believing it myself, but now I know. In a way I'm sorry you've forced me to do this, Drake. It makes me admit that I was completely wrong about you."

Almost casually Janney reached toward his pistol. Gardner made no move. He sat tight against the table, with his elbows on it, staring at Janney.

Vaughn raised his pistol. He sighted full on Janney's chest and pulled the trigger. Glass shards spewed across the room. With his gun in his hand Janney fell forward against the table, then rolled to the floor. The dog at Vaughn's feet let out a startled yelp.

Vaughn felt his way along the building. His pistol barrel struck the thin panel of a door. He threw it open and stepped inside. Gardner was still at the table. Janney was sprawled face down with his white hair spilled over his forehead on the dirty floor.

"You," Gardner said. "You earned five hundred." He put his head down on the table.

Vaughn shook him by the shoulder. "Get up! We've got to beat it!"

"Go away."

Vaughn put his pistol away and tried to lift Gardner to his feet. The weight was loose and shifting. "Come on!" Vaughn cried. The sight of Janney lying there was driving panic into him. He could not lift Gardner.

He was still trying when a fat man came into

the room, still fighting his arms through sus-
penders. His loose jowls were gray. There were
pockets under his eyes and the eyes themselves
were sagging toward half moons of redness.

Vaughn let go of Gardner and reached for his
pistol.

"You fool!" the fat man said. "I run this
place."

He turned Janney over, grunting when he saw
the sheet of blood smeared in the white hair
above Janney's ear, on down to the jaw. "Who's
he?" the saloonman muttered to himself. "I left
Drake here alone."

"Brett Janney. Five hundred dollars." Gardner's drunken laugh was a rasping sound.

"Dead?" Vaughn tried to swallow, but the
muscles of his throat knotted.

The saloonman knelt. "Hell no. He's bullet-
scorched along the side of his head, that's all.
Where did he come from?"

"York, Pennsylvania," Gardner said with
drunken gravity. "He was a guerilla leader
once."

"One of them, huh? A stinking bushwhacker."
The fat man stepped across Janney and took the
bottle of whiskey. He drank, cleared his throat,
and spat on the floor. "You did a miserable job
of shooting, bub," he said to Vaughn. "I could
beat that, and I've been three fourths drunk
ever since the war."

Janney lay like dead. Vaughn glanced at the
broken window. His nerves jumped when the
dog outside whined and scratched at the door.
"I've got to get him home right away. Janney
wasn't the only one."

"Five hundred dollars." Gardner laughed.

"How you going to move him?" the fat man asked.

"That's what I want to know." Gardner hit the table a slow, deliberate thump with his fist. He reached for the bottle. "Did I pay you, Tubby?"

Vaughn knocked the bottle off the table. He struck Gardner on the head with his pistol barrel. Gardner's hands and arms shot out across the table and his face went down in the whiskey rings.

"By God!" Tubby said. "That was short and sweet. Where's your horses, kid?"

"In front." Vaughn hoped so.

The saloonman took Gardner's feet and Vaughn held him by the arms. Tubby stumbled over Janney's legs and kicked at them when he regained balance. They carried Gardner out. Vaughn felt a great relief when he heard Mitch snort at the hitchrail.

The livery hostler's voice came carefully from the darkness. "What's going on, Tubby?"

"We just murdered four men and we're taking them out to bury them," the saloonman said. "Now you can go to bed in peace, Fellows."

CHAPTER 7
"Kill Brett Janney"

THEY PUT GARDNER ACROSS HIS SADDLE THE ONLY way he would fit, belly down. Tubby tied him there. It was well he did. Both horses crow-hopped in the morning cold before Vaughn got them lined out. The friendly dog went along.

Gardner began to groan and curse when the first dawn light touched the red hills. They were then a mile out of town and Vaughn had wandered off the trail into a scrub oak thicket. The whipping of the branches had stung Gardner back to life. He fell out of the saddle while Vaughn was trying to hold him and untie him at the same time.

Still utterly stupid, Gardner was on his feet when Vaughn saw the five riders trotting toward the town. His eyes went from them to the far dim breaks in the direction of Pennsylvania Creek, where Wagonwheel lay.

"You've got to ride," Vaughn said.

"Sure! I'll ride a nice fat battery horse up the hill, and we'll plant the pieces there and if they come at us in columns we'll string their intestines from tree to tree! And don't throw any water on the cannon this time, men!"

"Don't you remember anything?" Vaughn asked desperately.

"I remember falling out of a duck-boat once when I was a boy." Gardner laughed. He leaned against his horse. "Now there's a fine-looking dog. Where'd you get him?"

Vaughn helped him mount. Gardner raked his foot aimlessly, feeling for the right stirrup. His horse went out with a lunge. Gardner found the stirrup automatically then and habit made him bring the animal under control.

At last Vaughn got ahead of him. He led toward Cloverleaf, and then he remembered that Anson Dodge had been mentioned with Janney's other men, and the owners of Wagonwheel. He cursed the fact that he still knew little of the tensions and the undercurrents of the Spotted Hills, although he was involved.

Anxiously, he kept looking back. There seemed to be no pursuit, but Gardner was most unsteady in the saddle now, and getting worse. Another hour of riding and the sun was hot. The dog was panting, the horses lathered.

Gardner was still completely fogged with drunkenness, jerking from side to side every time he dozed and started to fall off his horse. As much as possible Vaughn kept to the troughs of the hills. The skyline offered nothing but waiting vastness, more hostile because there was no threat in sight; but the little valleys gave a feeling of security.

It was in one of them between two sandstone hills that Gardner half dismounted, half fell from his saddle. He muttered, "Far enough." He sprawled on the ground, asleep as soon as he struck. His pistol was gone, Vaughn noticed.

For a while Vaughn did not unsaddle the horses. He sat on a rock, waiting. The dog lay at his feet. When he decided that Gardner might sleep for hours, Vaughn stripped the saddles off and picketed the horses. He took his rifle and climbed one of the hills. He could see well in three directions but the hill across from him cut off his view toward Cloverleaf.

Danger would come, he told himself, from one of the visible areas; but after a while the thought did not satisfy him. He went to the other hill. Except by standing exposed on the very top he was confronted with another blind spot caused by the rise he had just left.

Very low and deep the growling came from Sport. Vaughn tried to go back to sleep, but the dog kept growling. Vaughn came to with a guilty start. "Quiet, quiet!" he whispered. Sport stopped growling, but he was stiff, with his heavy muzzle pointed across the little valley.

Oh, God! I've let them sneak in on us!

Only one man over there, a burly man coming down through the rocks with a pistol in his hand. His boots were off. Vaughn saw the dun color of his sox as the man's feet tested each rock as carefully as a cat would move its pads when stalking a bird. It was Anson Dodge.

"Dodge!" Vaughn yelled.

* * *

For a tick of time Dodge hesitated. He fired into the valley. The next bullet came at Vaughn, now standing shoulder high above the rocks. It sprayed fragments against the side of his neck. He did not flinch or lose his aim. Gardner had pounded that much into him. He shot across the little valley and saw Dodge fall. Loosely the Cloverleaf foreman rolled down the hill with his bootless feet scraping warm sandstone.

"Vaughn!" Gardner's cry carried concern that must have been jarred from deep inside him.

Vaughn raced down the hill. The dog took it as fun and leaped beside him, barking. Gardner was haggard and his eyes were red, but they were aware.

"I was awake," he said. "When you yelled I rolled clear. Was he alone?"

"I guess so."

Gardner went over to Dodge. Vaughn stayed where he was. When Gardner took the man's pistol belt Vaughn knew Dodge was dead. He did not want to see him.

When Gardner returned he asked, "Where are we?"

"Three or four miles from Cloverleaf, I think."

Gardner ran his hand across his forehead. "I can't remember much of anything. What happened?"

Vaughn told him.

"Let's get out of here. We'll go home. Maybe there's a day or two left." Gardner looked at the dog. "Where'd he come from?"

"Town. Last night."

"I wish I could remember something."

They rode toward the mountains.

Suddenly Gardner ripped open his shirt. He turned his horse toward Vaughn. "See that?" His chest was splashed with white scars. "I got that when I got my face. I was two years in a hospital. She married Lee Hester, but he knew I was alive. Martha is my daughter. I never saw her before I came out here to ruin Lee Hester.

"Then don't blame Molly! She thought I was dead. She married again. Martha thinks Lee Hester is her father. She loves him. The Hesters always had a way with women. When Molly saw me, fourteen years after I was supposed to have been killed, I wished I'd never let her see me.

"I settled up there against the mountains. Sometimes I walked the meadow all night, trying to figure out what to do. I decided to grind Lee Hester into the earth and claim what was mine. Janney knew it. He's as shrewd as a rat. He's always been on the fringe, waiting to dart in and snatch something.

"All that time I wouldn't let Molly make a clean break. I said it was because of Martha, but it was only because I wanted to torture Hester. It didn't work; he's too cold-blooded. He tortured me, instead."

Gardner shook his head. "I made everything worse. When I found out where Hester was, I should have come out here and killed him, or I shouldn't have come at all. Now the whole thing is tangled up in another mess. Did you hear anything Janney told me last night?"

"Yes," Vaughn said reluctantly. "I heard some things."

"When Janney first showed up in this country, I talked it over with him. I was going to smash Cloverleaf. Lee Hester doesn't own it but it means as much to him as if he did, because everyone thinks he owns it. Janney was going to take the ranch. There's no legal filing on any part of it.

"All I wanted was revenge, and my wife and daughter. Janney began to set his sights higher. He decided to take the whole Spotted Hills."

"The whole country!"

"It's nothing, compared with what men have taken in Texas and farther west. Smash Cloverleaf and Wagonwheel, and there's only a few small men left to fight. That cold devil, Finlay Hester, decided to do the same thing. All he had to do was break Wagonwheel.

"Lee wasn't big enough to do it, so Finlay tried to use Dodge." Gardner cursed. "You know what he promised Dodge, besides being foreman of the whole country? He promised him Molly. Dodge had been in love with her for years."

"I'm glad I killed him then," Vaughn said.

Gardner began to button his shirt. The sweat and whiskey odor of him was strong in the still warm air.

"Janney got wind of how Finlay was trying to use Dodge. Janney never misses anything. Stack a blind man sitting in a dark room, no matter how strong his will may be, against the clever talk of Brett Janney, backed with three ex-guerillas, and you can understand how Janney won Dodge by promising him the same things Finlay offered."

There were four, not three, with Janney; but the point did not matter now, Vaughn thought.

"You know what was supposed to happen

when Wagonwheel and Cloverleaf came to your
shack that night? Finlay planned it. Charley
Burgett and Troutt Warner were supposed to
have been wiped out in the dark. Dodge couldn't
do it. Before the men left Cloverleaf, Lee made
them leave their guns. Dodge sneaked a pistol
along, all right, but your father put up such a
scrap Dodge never got a chance to get at Warner
and Burgett.

"He did crawl in and shut the rifle down. I
know that, because he told Janney about it."

Dodge then. He was dead now. That was
enough for Vaughn. The knowledge that Anson
Dodge had killed Carmody Steele would help,
in time, to dull the tight, sick feeling Vaughn
felt each time he recalled a rifle shot across the
little valley of the two red hills. The vow he had
made to kill everyone who took part in the night
raid on the homestead was a childish thing to
him now.

"I drew Janney into the plan," Gardner said.
"I've got to live with that mistake, no matter
what happens. He played it two ways, like he
always did everything. He went to Wagonwheel
and told them there that Cloverleaf could be ruined and taken. The idea grew on Warner and
Burgett, especially after Anson Dodge testified
that Finlay Hester was planning the same thing
against Wagonwheel.

"You see what I started, Vaughn?"

It was clear enough to Vaughn Steele now.
Brett Janney had needed Gardner because he
feared him, and because Gardner's desires did
not conflict with Janney's. But now Janney was
done with Gardner. He would use, instead, the
force of Wagonwheel.

"Charley Burgett is a sneak," Gardner said. "Warner, I believe, could be made to live in peace here. He'll be the first one Max Sloss or Janney will kill after they have used him up against Cloverleaf."

Dodge was dead, taking much from Finlay Hester's strength, even though he had been a traitor to Hester. Lee Hester had laughed about the threat of Wagonwheel; he had said Burgett and Warner were his friends. There would be then, Vaughn reasoned, no trouble coming from Cloverleaf.

It would come the other way. But without Janney to foment it—

"How bad did you wound Janney?" Gardner asked.

"Tubby said it was a bullet scorch across the head."

"He won't be worth anything for a few days. There won't be any trouble until then, at least."

Vaughn went on with his reasoning. It was simple, if you had the stomach for it. Kill Brett Janney. Finlay Hester had a strong point there.

Vaughn said, "Kill Brett Janney."

"No!"

"Why not? It will stop what you started."

"No!"

"You said once you might not kill him even if he gave you an excuse. Last night he was going to shoot you. Why don't you want—"

"He's Molly's twin brother!"

CHAPTER 8
No Law

WHEN THEY REACHED GARDNER'S HORSE RANCH AT sundown Gardner swung down wearily. He stood for a moment looking down at the Spotted Hills, and then he went in and climbed into his bunk with his clothes on.

Drake Gardner was gone when Vaughn woke up. On the top of the cold stove was a note. *Stay here*.

He did not think of the dog until after breakfast. He whistled. The horses in the meadow pricked up their ears. The whistle rode away to silence. Sport was gone. Maybe back on the hill chasing rabbits. Why would Gardner take the dog with him?

Vaughn went scouting on the hill, pushing through rose thickets, whistling now and then. There was no use. Sport was gone. It left

Vaughn more uneasy than ever. He went back to the cabin.

"Hello, kid."

Vaughn's muscles jerked. Frog was standing near the stove, his thumbs hooked into his pistol belt, his puckered mouth grim, turned down at the corners. Vaughn squinted, trying to adjust to the sudden change of light.

"Where's Gardner?"

Vaughn went for his pistol. His hand was on the butt grips when Frog's weapon was clear, pointing at Vaughn's stomach.

"Take it easy," Frog said. "You trying to get killed, kid?"

Vaughn eased his hand away from his pistol. He glanced behind him, expecting to see Sloss stalking in, licking his red lips, expecting to see Janney's deep creased face all rutted in an evil grin.

"I'm alone," Frog said. "Promise not to get the drop on me again if I holster up?" His lips twitched.

"You scared the hell out of me. What do you want?"

"Where's Drake." Frog put his pistol away.

"I don't know."

"You sure?"

"I don't know where he is."

Frog considered. "My horse is down in the trees. I'm going to get him and take care of him. I'm not with Janney any more. That good enough for you, or will I see a rifle looking at me when I come back?" He grinned.

"I guess it'll do."

"You'll never buy a wooden nutmeg, will you?" Frog walked out and went toward the

trees below the cabin. He came back in a few
minutes with his horse. Vaughn put the corral
bars down. When they went into the cabin
again, Frog sat down as if he were weary. "No
idea where he is, huh?"

"Maybe Cloverleaf," Vaughn said cautiously.

"Yeah." Frog nodded. "I reckon. You mind if
I have something to eat? Been up all night." He
began to unstrap his pistol belt. "Funny thing,
I thought I was done with guns when the war
ended. It didn't work out that way."

"Guerilla?" Vaughn asked.

"No, by God! You know about Janney then?"

Vaughn nodded. He began to cook breakfast
for Frog. "How is Janney?"

"He's got a thousand dollar headache. Every
time he makes a quick move he closes his eyes
and cusses."

"How soon will he be all right?"

Frog shrugged. "I've seen men die from little
bullet cuts across the skull. Brett won't though.
You tried to crease him thataway?"

"I tried to hit him in the heart."

"That's a pistol for you." Frog drank three
cups of coffee before he began to eat. There was
an insouciant good humor about him. "Know
who killed your pa?"

Vaughn nodded.

"He won't hear the dogs bark no more, will
he?"

"You saw Dodge?"

"In my prowling around I sort of cut your
tracks." Frog glanced at Vaughn's rifle laid on
pegs on the wall. "I buried him. Any man ought
to get that. I'll bet Finlay Hester still thinks he's
the fair-haired boy."

Vaughn dumped bacon into a tin plate. "What's going to happen?"

Frog shrugged. "I ain't remaining to see. If Gardner comes back before dark I'll speak a word or two, and then—" Frog grinned "—I've got a cousin out in Oregon, or someplace such like, that I ain't seen in years."

Vaughn asked a question that had disturbed some basic feeling in him for a day and night. "How can one bunch of men just kill off some others and grab everything they own? How can that work out?"

"You stayed mighty close to that plow, didn't you, Steele? Your pa could have answered that. You ought to be able to answer it yourself, seeing as what happened one night to your house down there on Elk Run."

Vaughn supposed he had known the answer all the time; it was just that knowing was a shock. The things you learned at home didn't fit the pattern of the world around you, maybe.

Frog puffed the pipe. He did not sleep.

Sport arrived, bursting into the cabin.

"He'll be down there in the trees," Frog said. "He'll be wondering about the tracks of my horse. Save him the scout in, Steele."

Vaughn found Gardner easing toward the cabin through the edge of the trees. "Frog's horse made the tracks, Vaughn. Was Frog on it?"

Vaughn nodded.

"I told the dog to stay here," Gardner said. "He caught up with me about two miles away. Now that's a habit you'd best break him of."

Frog was still on the bunk. He sat up and knocked the dottle from his pipe on the side pole, studying Gardner's face. "No luck, huh? I'd say you went to Cloverleaf."

"Lee is a crazy fool," Gardner said. "He wouldn't believe that such a thing could happen. He still thinks he's in Pennsylvania. He also told me that I was trying to make a hero of myself before his wife, and then he laughed in my face."

"Little Gentle Face?" Frog asked.

"I had bad luck there. He sat there weighing what I'd told him with that dreamy, creepy look. I'd left my pistol on the porch. That blamed carved orangewood handle on Dodge's gun caught Nan's eye. She called clear across the yard to Martha, 'Why, Mr. Gardner's got Mr. Dodge's gun, the one with the big stars on the handle!' "

"A man ought to have two pistols," Frog murmured.

"You didn't turn around when you walked out, I see," Frog said.

"I remembered. He used to go out at night with that knife, looking for Rebel pickets. He was an artillery captain, Frog, but he went out alone, and when he came back grinning he would say, 'You know, the nights grow quieter around here all the time, Gardner.'

"No, I didn't turn my back, Frog. I opened the door and stepped against the wall of the room, inside. The knife went stomach-high through the doorway. When he heard it hit the wall in the hallway he shook his head. He said, 'Toss it over toward my feet, Drake, so the children won't see it. I might have known you wouldn't trust even a poor sightless man.' "

"Crazy?" Frog said in a hushed voice.

Gardner shook his head. "A Hester, that's all."

"Yeah," Frog said. "I've heard of the cousins."

"When does Janney start it?" Gardner asked.

Frog grinned. "When I get back from scouting to see if Lee still has everybody out on spring roundup."

"Would you take that chance and go back? Maybe we could fix up something for them to ride into."

Frog shook his head. "Not for the biggest farm in all Ohio, Drake. Brett has been smiling at me too easy ever since the time I sneaked in here alone last spring. I've got a cousin that needs seeing. He may be in China now."

"No, you can't go back," Gardner said. He felt the coffee pot, and then poured himself a cup. His eyes showed that his mind was working now with all the webs of indecision cleared away. Vaughn was pleased, and scared.

"There's women there," Gardner said. "They wouldn't leave, not Molly and Martha, at least."

"I'm marked," Frog said.

"I wouldn't promise you a thing."

"I didn't ask."

"Not a single thing."

"I'll be in the pass by morning," Frog said.

"You've gone this far."

"Just on my way out, Drake. Brett ran thin on me a long time ago, but I'm still afraid of him."

"The kid was afraid of Dodge, too," Gardner said.

"I know. I came by that place." Frog grinned. "Steele started to draw on me too."

Gardner groaned. "I'll leave you home, Vaughn, when we ride away from here."

"We?" Frog asked. "Who said—"

"Would you like to see Sloss loose with those women, Frog?" The scars on Gardner's cheek were livid.

"Next to Janney, I'd like to see Sloss dead," Frog said. "But—"

"Two days after I enlisted bushwhackers killed my whole family," Gardner said. "It wasn't Janney's bunch. This was in Missouri. I've never tried to get even with the breed. Don't you think it's time? I need help, Frog."

Frog rubbed his broad bald head. "That's getting it sort of down to where I can understand it. By morning I should be in the pass . . . How do I know I could ever get through the country on the other side, anyway? They're looking day and night over there for anybody that ever rode with Brett."

Now there were three of them, Vaughn thought.

Gardner asked, "When will he try it?"

"Dawn. Noon. Dusk. Brett never got in no rut thataway."

"I'm not long on ammunition," Gardner said.

Frog grinned. "It so happens that I borrowed a scad of cartridges of various kinds just before I left the Wagonwheel. I thought, Drake, that you might put up some kind of hard-luck story to make me change my mind. I'm not fooling though, my intentions were ninety-eight per cent to go over the hill."

CHAPTER 9
Job for Sloss

LEE HESTER PACED HIS BROTHER'S ROOM AT CLOverleaf. "No," he said, "you're wrong, Finlay. For all that Brett is no good, he still wouldn't do it. And Gardner has a soft streak. He's a weak fool. That cannon burned more than the face off him. No man with any guts would have put up with what I've given him."

"Dodge is dead, Lee. Gardner killed him."

"Oh, hell. Dodge said he might be gone several days when I sent him out to ride the south breaks. This is a big country, Finlay. You can't realize—"

"I see it better than you do," Finlay said softly. "You didn't send Dodge to ride for cattle. I sent him to find Drake Gardner and kill him. You've never sent Dodge any place, Lee. When are you going to understand that?"

"Your stinking money!" Lee said savagely.

"What good is it to you? One day you'll misjudge the steps when you start out to the lattice house—"

"Be quiet, Lee. I can't see your face. I can't see that handsome shell you use to impress the people of this country. The whine in your voice is enough for me, even if I did not know you. I want you to go to Wagonwheel and talk to Troutt Warner. Patch up a peace someway. Show him that he can't trust Janney. Get me some time, Lee. I'll send for men I know, men that I can trust. Get me time, Lee, and then I'll take this whole country."

Lee Hester stopped pacing. "What do we want with the whole country? You don't mean—"

"I've been patient with you, Lee. I've tried to teach you certain facts about our neighbors. They hate us. Their voices have told me that. They would do to us just what I've planned to do to them."

"Warner and Burgett?" Lee's voice was loud, incredulous.

"Close the door please, and lock it." Finlay listened carefully while his orders were being carried out. "Burgett particularly. He's a coward, Lee. Warner is not, but neither is he ruthless. I think he can pull Burgett out of this thing, at least for a time. That leaves Janney. Drake Gardner can stop him. Talk to Warner, then see Gardner. Tell Drake that you have decided to give up Molly, that you have realized she loves him."

"You're crazy, Finlay!"

"Tell him that Molly loves him, and that you have realized it at last. That will appeal to the softness in Drake. Add, of course, that you must have Gardner's help to smash this threat against Cloverleaf before you can release Molly.''

"That would be a filthy bargain! She doesn't love him. She's sorry for him, that's all!"

"You poor blind fool," Finlay murmured.

There was a long silence. "What makes you think she does?" Lee asked.

"She loves him, be sure of that," Finlay said. "Martha is the only reason that she has not left with him long ago. I recall the first day Gardner came here, from the dead, Molly thought. My ears see coloring in speech and hesitations. You wouldn't remember how Molly acted. Your own voice was trembling with fear that day, until you realized that Gardner had not come to kill you."

"Damn you, Finlay!"

"Ah, the truth is at last blooming."

"No! You've made it up, sitting here in the dark."

"I see no dark, Lee. You do." Finlay took a glass of water from the table at his side.

"There's foodstains all over your shirt and on your lapels," Lee said. "You're filthy. I suppose you can see that too."

Finlay shook his head. "Now I know there are three children who come into my room, and you are more child than the other two. It's a pity that I must use you to do the work of a man, but it must be that way for a while."

Lee tried to make his voice crisp, decisive. "I've got to get back to the men on the range." He walked across the room and let the shade up viciously. The sunlight struck on Finlay's pink face, but he did not flinch or turn his head.

"So you did not order the men back here, as I told you to do?"

Lee was looking at the lattice house. "No. I saw no need. You can ride out and do that, if it's so vital. You'd look good on a horse, Finlay."

He strode over to his brother. "I'll take that precious knife of yours, I think." Leaning past his brother, he opened the drawer in the little table.

"A quarrel is never good," Finlay said. He put his left hand on Lee's shoulder, gripping gently. His right hand pulled a pistol from under his coat. He shot Lee Hester in the side of the head at point-blank range.

The pistol was in Lee's hand where he lay sprawled beside an overturned table when Finlay unlocked the door in response to Molly Hester's knocks and calls. Finlay caught her shoulder as she started to go past him.

"Lee shot himself, Molly. He realized at last that you were still in love with Drake."

He could not see the horror on her face, but she did not start or gasp. Her silence told him what she believed. She whispered, "You killed him, Finlay!" She tried to thrust past him into the room.

"Go get the cook," he said. He pushed Molly Hester from the room. "Get the cook, I say!" He heard the girls running toward him. He closed the door behind him.

"Mother, what—"

"Don't go near him!" Molly cried.

"Martha, Nan, come here." Finlay groped for

the wall. He knew exactly where it was. He heard Mrs. Hester run from the house.

Nan asked, "What happened, Uncle Finlay?"

"Nan, do you know where the men are?"

"I heard Uncle Lee say they were hunting cows in the cedar breaks on Kincaid Creek, but I don't know—I heard a shot, Uncle Finlay. What—"

"Tell her where the Cedar Breaks are, Martha. Go there, Nan. Tell the men to come back here at once. Martha, ride to Drake Gardner's place. Tell him to come here immediately."

There was silence. Then Martha said, "What was wrong with my mother, Uncle Finlay?"

He read hostility that had never been in her voice before. In a way it pained him, because he respected women as gentle, loving beings. That had always been a Hester weakness, and the Hesters were proud of it.

"She will tell you when you return," he said.

Martha said, "I won't go unless my mother tells me to. And neither is Nan going any place."

Mrs. Hester returned with the cook.

"I have told the children they must go do certain errands, Molly," Finlay Hester said. "Please add your approval."

"Yes, go," Mrs. Hester said. "Go now!"

When the front door banged shut, Finlay stood back and extended his arm toward his room.

In late afternoon Brett Janney lay on warm grass on a hill a mile from Cloverleaf, with his hat shading his eyes. Charley Burgett sat near him. With one hand Burgett kept pulling blistered skin from his cheekbones; with the other hand he pulled blades of grass, rolling them between his thumb and forefinger before he dropped them. His deep-set eyes drifted frequently to Janney.

Four men waited near the horses, two riders from Wagonwheel and two of Janney's men.

"Nervous?" Janney asked of Burgett.

"Yeah. About Warner."

"When it's done, he'll have to go along."

"What about Gardner?"

Janney sat up. "He's paid for. Him and the kid." He looked at the men squatted near the horses. The two from Wagonwheel were not much, according to his way of thinking. His own men, Rance and Sloss, would do; but a gang wore out. It was best to make frequent changes.

Sloss was a sore spot. It was best to get him killed, if it could be arranged. Sloss couldn't remember that the old guerilla days were dead. He would run wild among the women at Cloverleaf and that would not do out here.

With a wondering sort of detachment Janney thought that one of the women was his sister, and another his niece.

Yes, Sloss was worn out as far as Janney was concerned.

Burgett kept watching Janney uneasily.

It was possible that Charley Burgett would also get killed in the fight. As the brother of the woman whose husband had owned Cloverleaf, Brett Janney would feel rather bad about the raid Wagonwheel had made. Once he was well set up at the ranch, he would have to see that Wagonwheel paid for killing his brother-in-law.

"What are you grinning about?" Burgett asked.

"About living like a king, after all the years of abuse I've taken."

"The little ranches—we won't have to get so rough there, will we?" Burgett asked.

"They'll run, if we work it right. Half their range for me, half for you, with whatever happens to be loose on it. That's all right, isn't it, Burgett?"

"Yeah." About one fourth more of the Spotted Hills. Burgett could move then, make the break with Warner, and then he could lay other plans. Everything else was all right, except . . . He looked uneasily at Janney again.

"This is the worst of it," Janney said. "After that we'll move more subtly. You and I can own the hills, Burgett. We need each other. We'll have to get along, won't we?"

They did need each other, but Janney's stating the fact seemed to color it a little. White-haired at his age. Maybe he had taken a lot of abuse from the world. Cloverleaf would seem like a lot to him, and he ought to be satisfied with it. But that damned crawling grin of his . . .

One of the Wagonwheel men said, "There's a horse coming, Burgett!" He started up the hill.

Burgett took some assurance from the fact that the man had addressed him, and not Janney.

Piney Bauman rode in a few minutes later. He was a wiry little man with a pinched face, and he could smell out loot in a poor-white shack. He was the only one of Janney's bunch that Janney trusted. A gold bracelet, a few rings, and a gambling game were enough to satisfy Piney Bauman. He rode directly to Janney and swung down.

"The hands are still away, Brett, all but the cook. On the way back I scouted the house. The two girls—"

"What about Gardner?"

"They skipped," Bauman said. "All three. You was right. Frog had been there."

"How do you know they skipped?" Janney asked.

"They took everything in the cabin that was worth a dime. They druv the horses ahead of them and lit out toward the pass."

"How far did you follow?"

"Two mile, I reckon. They never let a horse get away, Brett." Piney took a chew of tobacco. He offered some to Burgett, who shook his head. "They skipped, Brett. They wouldn't bother with the horses, otherwise, would they?"

Janney chewed his lip. His eyes narrowed. He was so full of tricks himself he could not trust the news.

"That helps," Burgett said.

Bauman ignored him. "I burned the cabin."

"You fool!" Janney said. "I could have used that as a line camp." Almost in the same breath he added, "Me and Burgett could have used it."

"I didn't know." Bauman's hand was on a broken watch in his pocket, the nearest thing to any item of value he had been able to find in Gardner's cabin.

"You couldn't dig out any loot," Janney said, "and that's when you always start pouring coal oil."

"No, Brett—"

"What was it you started to say about the girls?" Janney asked.

"The big one rode toward the mountains. The

other one went skimming off to the south a while ago. I just seen one man, the cook, around the ranch."

"Lee's there," Janney said. "I saw him myself a couple of hours ago." Finlay would be there too, of course. The idea of shooting an afflicted man disturbed Janney more than he would have admitted. That would be a job for Sloss. He rose. "We'll ride in just like any visitors. How long ago were those tracks made above Gardner's place, Piney?"

"Sometime yesterday, early."

"I'd like it better if they'd been made today."

While the group was mounting Janney had a few quick words with Sloss alone.

CHAPTER 10
Nothing to Put
Your Back Against

FROM AN ASPEN THICKET ON TOP OF BUFFALO HILL,
about two miles from Cloverleaf, Gardner, Frog
and Vaughn watched the last of the smoke die
against the mountains.

"I'll build it again," Gardner said. "This time
without the extra bunks."

The waiting built up terrible pressure in
Vaughn. "Hadn't we better get on down there?"

"Not yet," Gardner said. "Wait until we see
which direction Bauman takes."

The little rider on a powerful claybank had
passed sometime before, going toward Cloverleaf. Gardner had said nothing would happen
until after he went back to report to Janney.
Frog agreed, but Vaughn wondered how they
could be sure. He kept patting Sport. He kept
thinking of Max Sloss.

Vaughn was the first one to see the rider streaking toward the mountains. "Oh, oh!" he said. It came out a whisper, although the rider was a quarter of a mile off.

"That's a woman," Frog said.

"Martha." Gardner looked at Vaughn. "She might be headed for my place. Go after her, Vaughn, and then stay with her. Stay clear of Cloverleaf too."

"You didn't want me along in the first place!"

"That's right. Don't come near Cloverleaf until you know for sure how things stand. Go on now. She's running the legs off that sorrel."

Gardner and Frog rode on. Vaughn hesitated. Gardner did not look back, and that, more than anything, convinced the youth that he must follow orders.

She rode all the faster when she saw him coming. It was a long chase before he got within hailing distance and she recognized his voice. Her face was pale and sweating and her hair was in disorder. "Where's Drake Gardner?"

Vaughn jerked his hand toward Cloverleaf. "Have they come in yet?"

"They?"

"Oh hell! I'm sorry. I mean—What do you want with Drake?"

"My uncle wants him. I think—" She slid down from the saddle and leaned against the sorrel and began to sob. "Something's happened to my father! I know it. Something awful is going on at home!"

She took him by the shortest route to Cloverleaf, and they let the horses stretch out. He left her and Sport in a scrub oak thicket.

He saw then why he was not too late. Two riders were coming from the south toward a group of men on a hill. Janney must have sent scouts toward the Cedar Breaks before he came to a full decision. From the ranchhouse the group upon the rise would not be visible. Vaughn watched the scouts report.

Only three men came down the hill, riding casually. By the black beard, one was Max Sloss; another, tall, slope-shouldered, was Charley Burgett. The third one Vaughn did not know.

Vaughn held to the trees until he reached the lattice house. He crawled from there to the back door of the ranchhouse. It was locked. he dared not risk the pounding and shouting it would take to attract someone's attention. He ran through the soft soil of a flower bed to Finlay Hester's window. The shade was full drawn. The window swung back when he pushed. He hauled himself astraddle the sill and eased inside. It was gloomy and the hallway door was shut. He was tiptoeing across the room when he saw the sheet-covered lump upon the bed.

Every nerve jerked in his body. He half turned to run back to the window; and then with icy sweat on his brow, he saw Drake Gardner standing on a chair, peering from a narrow casement window near the fireplace in the living room.

Terror gave way to normal fear. He ran down the hall. Two pistols and a rifle trained on him. There were four men, Gardner, Frog, the cook, and Finlay Hester, who said "Ah, the clodhopper boy I would judge by the steps."

Gardner jerked back to the window. "At the

cook shack now. Where's Martha, damn you, Steele!''

''Hidden.''

''They see there's no one here,'' Gardner said. ''They're riding into the yard. Don't shoot. We've got to have the whole bunch, or the surprise is worthless.''

''It ain't no surprise, or he would've come down hisself,'' Frog said. ''By God, what'll we do?''

Max Sloss hailed from the yard. ''Hello, the house! Anybody home?''

''if any of us go out—'' Gardner looked at Vaughn and Frog. He glanced at the cook. The man was sunk in terror now. He clutched his rifle and kept looking toward the kitchen.

''Is they anybody home?'' Sloss called.

''That's a southern voice.'' The calmness of Finlay Hester's tone did not conceal hatred. ''I'll bring those others into range for you, Drake. How many in the yard?''

''Three,'' Gardner said. ''They'll kill you if you step out there.''

''They wouldn't shoot a blind man. Are they near the porch steps?''

''Just getting off their horses,'' Frog said. ''Sloss would shoot his mother, mister.''

''Oh, I think not.'' Finlay Hester walked to the door. His fingertips touched the edge of a small table on the way and that was the only guidance he used. He took a cane from a hatrack. He opened the door, calling, ''Just a moment, gentlemen. Who is it?''

Vaughn was on his knees near Frog, peering from between a lace curtain and the casing of the window. He saw Finlay lose his steadiness. The man went out on the porch feeling with his cane ahead of him. He groped for the bannister of the porch and found it.

"Blind as a bat," Sloss said. All three of them were on the ground, at the foot of the steps. Sloss' hand was near his pistol. He relaxed a trifle. His red lips blossomed in his beard as he grinned.

Finlay leaned on the bannister. He hooked his cane over it. He was not bearing much weight on it, Vaughn observed. "Would the rest of you gentlemen speak up please?" Finlay asked.

"Burgett. You know me."

"Ah, yes, of course. You came to see Lee? He isn't home right now, but won't you come in anyway?"

"Well . . ." Burgett looked at Sloss.

"There's three of you. Would the third gentleman please speak?"

"I'm just a rider for Charley," the third man said.

"Burgett!" Finlay said.

"What?"

"Sloss?"

"Yeah?" Sloss scowled, puzzled.

"You rider, what's your name?"

"Leason."

Finlay's head had moved just a trifle as each man answered. Watching, Vaughn felt a fearful force of cunning evil in the man. He saw exactly what Finlay was doing.

"You alone here?" Sloss growled.

"Oh, yes." Finlay's weight had not been on the rail at all. His right hand went under his coat. He fired with the pistol close to his body,

guided by the uncanny wisdom of his ears. He
fired as they had spoken, from left to right.

Sloss reeled back with both hands on his
stomach. Burgett doubled in the middle and
dropped on the steps. Leason, the Wagonwheel
rider, saved his life by not trying to fight back.
He was near the rail. He jumped aside. The bullet meant for him went under the belly of a
horse.

The third shot sent back to Finlay's ears no
brutal impact sound. The plunging of the horses
ruined his aim. He made a guess as to which
way Leason had jumped; he fired, on the wrong
side. Leason touched his own pistol, and then
in panic he ran to his horse and leaped on. Finlay heard part of it, but he made another mistake.

He killed a horse ten feet from Leason. The
rider steadied then. He took careful aim from
his saddle. He fired. Finlay Hester dropped his
pistol. This time it was no pretense when he
leaned upon the bannister. He sank to his knees,
still clinging to the railing, and then he spilled
over on his side.

Leason spurred away.

Vaughn started to run toward the door, his
only thought to get a shot at the fleeing man.
Frog tripped him. Gardner leaped across the
room and wrenched the cook's rifle from him,
just as the man, standing now, was steadying to
fire through the window at Leason.

"You're trying to ruin it!" Gardner cried.

The cook and Vaughn steadied then, looking
shamefaced at each other. The cook was a full
grown man, Vaughn thought; he should have
known how to control himself.

Frog winked at Vaughn. "No hard feelings for this trip?"

Vaughn shook his head. It would take a lifetime to learn anything.

"That did it," Gardner said. "They're coming now."

"That Finlay almost made a sweep," Frog said. "Didn't that chill the red-hot vinegar in you?"

Gardner cursed. "Janney's holding back."

Frog said, "He always does."

One of the men at the foot of the steps gave a bubbling groan. All at once the cook was as sick and as frightened as before. "Will Mrs. Hester be all right alone in the cellar?"

Frog laughed. "Sure, pothook."

Only two men came into Vaughn's sight, Bauman and Leason. Janney was not trusting the evidence on the porch, what Finlay had said, or the silent house.

Gardner looked at Frog and pointed toward the kitchen. "Take the cook with you."

Frog and the cook crawled across the floor and disappeared.

"Leg shots," Gardner said. "Take Bauman."

The two men in front were on the ground, with pistols drawn. Remembering how Leason had rested his gun across his arm to shoot down Finlay Hester, Vaughn disobeyed another order. He aimed at Leason's leg as the man came toward the porch.

The big window came apart. Black powder smoke from his heavy rifle swirled back and blinded Vaughn. When he could see, Leason was on the ground. Bauman had ducked like a weasel under his horse and now he was running beside the animal, with it between him and the house.

While Vaughn was trying to reload, Gardner jumped to the chair at the narrow window by the fireplace. The window blew out in his face. He fell back on the floor with blood running from his forehead.

Vaughn dropped his rifle and ran to him.

"Hang onto your gun!" Gardner said. He wiped his arm across his face and got up. "That was Janney, from the corner of the cookshack."

A rifle and a pistol roared in the kitchen. Frog said, "Too bad, Rance." An instant later bullets crashed into the partition between the living room and kitchen. The cook cried out in pain.

"Oh hell!" Frog said. "Use the other arm."

"I can't see Janney now," Gardner said. "I think he got past the cook house and came this way."

There was utter silence. Vaughn's face was white as he watched Leason out there in the yard. He wanted to go out and help the man, but he knew he would not.

Frog yelled, "Bauman's skipping!" His pistol sounded twice. "Hang that Piney! He's no bigger than a flea." He shot once more. "He's clear. I always said he could duck a bullet."

"Stay here," Gardner said to Vaughn. He walked out the front door. For a moment he stood looking at Finlay Hester, and then he went down the steps.

Leason heard the sounds. He raised his head a little. "Will somebody help me now?"

Gardner went past him, carrying his pistol at his side. He did not slow down when the corner of the house no longer obscured his vision of the end wall. He turned that way to go around the next corner.

A heavy bay horse, dragging its reins and shying sidewise, started up the hill from somewhere near the corral. An instant later Brett Janney broke from behind a building and ran toward it. The second Wagonwheel man was escaping on foot.

"Janney!" Gardner called.

Vaughn shot the horse through the neck as Janney was reaching to catch the reins. The white-haired man, still half crouched from his attempt to grab the reins, turned toward Gardner.

Vaughn watched the running out of something that affected him like the chilling flow of Finlay Hester's voice; but he knew there was justice in this present act, somewhere.

Gardner kept walking with his pistol at his side. Janney leveled his own pistol, holding it, not firing. The attempt to rush Gardner backfired on Janney's nerves. He backed up a few steps, as if he would suddenly turn and run.

Gardner kept pacing toward him. He would get killed! Vaughn fumbled for a cartridge, but his eyes were on the hill, and he tried the wrong pocket.

Suddenly Janney dropped to one knee. He fired three times as fast as his pistol would work. Drake Gardner never broke stride. He raised his pistol slowly.

Vaughn cut his face on a shard of glass as he jerked when the rifle blasted beside him. The cook was kneeling at the window, and Frog was standing behind him; and Vaughn had heard neither of them come into the room.

Brett Janney seemed to sink into the ground. He rolled over on his face, and Gardner let his pistol drop until it was pointing toward the ground again.

"I got one of them!" the cook yelled. "And me with a bullet in my arm!"

Troutt Warner came in with Nan and the Cloverleaf riders an hour after sundown. His big mouth was loose and startled when he heard the story. "I won't lie," he said. "I figured to squeeze the Hesters out, but not like Janney and Burgett planned. When I found out what they were up to I streaked like hell to find Lee's crew. Lee's dead, too?"

Nan began to cry. Vaughn took her to the cookshack. There were a lot of things here that were none of his business. Let her think that Finlay Hester had been a kind and gentle man; let Martha mourn Lee as a father, until Molly and Gardner told her otherwise, if they ever did.

THE BIG TROUBLE

CHAPTER 1
War Trail

HE CRIES SAW HIS FIRST WHITE MEN AT THE END OF the summer of many rains. Big Elk, his father, had taken his family far from the main camp of the Uncompahgre Utes for the fall hunting, and now the lodge was set in the aspens at the head of a big park with never summer mountains hard against the night sky.

Ai, it was good to sit by the fire and think of the buffalo he would kill tomorrow. He Cries fondled his juniper bow and the straight arrows of currant wood in their bear hide quiver that his uncle, Jingling Thunder, had made for him that summer after the big fight with Arapahoes at Red Mountain. He Cries had never killed a buffalo, but here by the fire with his stomach full of antelope meat and with a warm drowsy feeling coming out of the night to him, He Cries was killing many buffalo.

He had seen the scattered herds that afternoon when he stole after his father, who had gone to hunt. But something had changed Big Elk's mind. Watching from a hill, He Cries had seen his father suddenly veer away from stalking a small herd of cows and ride straight toward the mountains. So He Cries followed to see what game tracks had taken Big Elk away from the buffalo.

It was tracks of men, five of them. They did not wear moccasins, which seemed very strange to He Cries. They wore something else that crushed the grass and left sharp edges in soft ground. He Cries followed, fascinated, until Big Elk reached from the ambush of a spruce thicket and grabbed him by the breechclout.

He Cries was not caught entirely unaware, for he had seen where Big Elk leaped aside from the trail, and so the son had time to set an arrow and half draw his bow. That was fairly good; otherwise Big Elk would have ignored his son for several days as punishment for carelessness. Big Elk asked, looking at the trail, "How many?"

"Five. They wear strange moccasins."

"They do," Big Elk said. "Go back to the lodge." His face was dark, so that He Cries was sure it was time to go.

Now Big Elk sat by the fire silent with the darkness behind his eyes, such as the times after coming from councils where he had shaken his head at Arrow, sub chief of the Uncompahgre Utes, who was no friend of Big Elk or his brother Jingling Thunder.

He Cries' mother and her mother were singing the night song of the leaves, not loud, for that would not have been well, with Big Elk looking so darkly at the fire. He Cries moved a little closer to his grandmother. Old Running Woman, captured as a child from the Cheyennes long ago, was not like other old women who let their buckskin skirts grow black with blood and grease, who said only sharp words to those who married their daughters, and who were forever complaining that the hunting had been better long ago.

Running Woman's buckskins were clean and white, like those of He Cries' mother. She raised her voice when there were things to say, and she said them without fear, so that even Big Elk listened.

And now she ceased her singing and said across the fire, "What is it, my son?"

Big Elk looked at her half angrily. He did not like it when she read his mind and asked questions before he chose to speak. Her daughter was getting the habit too, Big Elk often complained. There would be no peace in a man's lodge when he was old. He scowled at both women and then looked at the fire again.

But Running Woman was old, and her face had been black painted many times for sons and nephews who came back dead across their ponies. She was old and had seen many things, and so a scowl did not bother her.

"Did you see the marks today of those with tattoos on the breast?" she asked.

Big Elk answered because he knew he would have to answer sooner or later. "The Arapahoes are gathered now in camps for hunting on the plains. They will not be in the mountains." He glanced at He Cries. "No, old woman, I did not see the marks of the Arapahoes."

He Cries felt his mother's hand touch him, then push against him gently. It was time for him to go into the lodge. The others would talk then about what Big Elk had seen this day. He Cries did not care. He was too sleepy. Tonight in his dreams he had many buffalo to kill, and tomorrow . . . perhaps . . .

His mother's hand ran down his back, patted him on the thigh as he moved away. Both she and Running Woman watched him go, but when he glanced back from the lodge flap, yawning, the three at the fire were staring at each other solemnly.

They had cloudy thoughts, He Cries thought. They did not seem to know that dark things which sometimes troubled the mind at night all passed away before the morning sun stood bright on the forests and the mountains.

Terrible thunder jarred He Cries from his robes. He sat up, frightened. There was no whispering rain against the hides of the lodge, and the flaps were not tied. It could not be raining.

From outside he heard Big Elk grunt deep in his chest. The thunder came again, so loud, so close that He Cries clapped his hands to his ears. And then he heard strange voices running rapidly in an unknown tongue. His mother cried out fiercely. Running Woman began to sing. The grunts and blows of a sharp, brief struggle came to He Cries.

He crept to the lodge flaps and looked out. Big Elk was lying on his face by the fire, and the fire showed the bright streams running from two holes in his back. A man all covered with clothes was looking down at Big Elk, in his hands a long brown club that smoked. The smell of the brown club had drifted clear to the lodge, filling He Cries' nostrils with a bitter smell.

There were five of the men whose bodies were covered. Their faces were hairy, and by that He Cries knew they were what the old ones called white men. Three of them had the big sticks that smoked. Two were holding He Cries' mother on the ground.

Antelope meat was scattered on a buffalo robe near broken cooking vessels. They had eaten, these strangers with hairy faces, and then they had killed Big Elk. He Cries was filled with terror, but he half rose, ready to leap from the lodge, and then he heard what Running Woman was singing.

Run, He Cries, run away.
  Big Elk is dead.
Run quick, run far, He Cries.
  Run to Jingling Thunder.

He Cries' mother began to struggle again, twisting against the hands that held her. She spat into one of the hairy faces. The man struck her as one kills a rabbit with his hand, and she lay still.

"Run quick, run far . . ." the old woman chanted.

One of the men turned toward the lodge, speaking sharply in the strange tongue. The hair upon his face was as red as mountains that had just hidden the sun, and it seemed to He Cries that his eyes were red also when they saw the figure crouched at the flaps. The man raised the brown club, grinning, with firelight strong on big white teeth.

From under the wide fold of her skirt Running Woman snatched the juniper bow that He Cries had left beside her. She strung an arrow swiftly. The bow made a little thump and the man with sunset in the hair of his face shouted. He dropped his brown club and grabbed his arm, tearing at the arrow.

Running Woman started to set another little arrow. "Run, He Cries," she said.

The awful thunder came once again before Running Woman could draw the small bow. Her head went low upon her chest and red blossomed on the white of her beaded dress.

He Cries ran with a sob in his chest. He wormed under the hide wall away from the fire and darted into the aspens. Two of the hairy faces came after him, crashing hard with their strange moccasins. In terror He Cries ran, forgetting everything Big Elk had taught him.

The white men sent their thunder after him. It reached out and knocked He Cries into a bush, filling his head with a great brilliance. But that was what saved him. He lay still then, holding one hand against his head where only part of an ear remained. The white men crashed close to him, shouting to each other, but he lay still, crouched like a snowshoe rabbit. After a while they went back to the lodge.

Just once as he was slipping away, quietly now, he heard his mother cry out. The last he heard was the loud laughter of the hairy faces.

He was naked in the cold night with the never

summer mountains black around him. His head was still ringing from the thunder sticks, and the injured side was hurting. He whimpered a little.

It was at least one sun to where he had last seen Jingling Thunder's lodge, two suns to the main camp. He Cries swam a big beaver pond. He tore his legs on roots when he scrambled out on the far bank, and then he trotted through the tall grass, never doubting that he was going in the right direction.

He would remember till the day of the big sunset this night when he had seen his first white men.

He Cries was then five summers old.

His name was White Bear, after the great hunch-shouldered grizzly, the summer the Arrow's people camped on the slopes below the mountain of the snow woman. The boy who had been He Cries was gone, vanished with the little whimpers he had made thirteen summers before when he ran through the night from miners who had killed his family.

The wedge of dark brown hair that ran into a braid on the right side of his head did not hide his mangled ear. There were other scars on him now, for he had taken six scalps from the Tattooed Breasts. The blood of the tall Cheyennes had carried strongly down to him from Running Woman. He was lighter than the other Utes and taller by two hand spans than the average.

Today he was going to raise his voice in council.

Jingling Thunder came from his lodge, followed by his sons, Red Cow and Soldier. Strong of frame, almost black-skinned, Jingling Thunder had the same quick-fixing gaze that was all White Bear could now remember of his father. The years had not hardened Jingling Thunder's joints or put a film on his eyes. He could still ride hard and see a flick of movement miles ahead, just as long ago when he had ridden in one day from the headwaters of the Arkansas to the big white man's town upon the plains, trailing five hairy faces who had taken Big Elk's ponies.

White Bear's mother had been dead when Jingling Thunder reached the lodge at *Bayou Salade*. They were all dead; but White Bear's mother had not died a good death, and that had left a terrible bitterness against all white men in her son. The bitterness was shared by Jingling Thunder, who had missed catching up with the five by no more than the flight of two long arrows.

Jingling Thunder sent a wicked look toward the huge lodge of the Arrow. There were two white men in there now, messengers from their big chief. The sides were not rolled up to catch the cool air, which was the case too often when white men came to talk to the Arrow.

"They say one thing to the Arrow. In council he says another thing to us." Red Cow spat. He sent an angling look through the pinions to where Shavano, war chief of the tribe, sat before his lodge with a sullen fierceness on his face.

"The white men promise things to Arrow, but they are not the promises we hear from him." Soldier spat and looked at White Bear.

"Silence," Jingling Thunder said. "You voices

are like the pinion birds." His face said that they spoke truth.

Red Cow and Soldier were warriors. They had ridden many times beside White Bear against the Arapahoes and the Striped Arrow people. They had been far south and brought back ponies and scalps from the Navajos. But their father's words kept them silent for a little while.

Then Red Cow spoke again. "The white men who wash the river sands and dig holes in the rocks are slipping back across the mountains every day."

"The last big party that the Arrow took to the pass went only a short distance after he pointed eastward and said, 'Go.' Now they are traveling toward the San Juan once more." Soldier grunted. "That is the white man's way of keeping his promise."

"I know these things. Be silent." Jingling Thunder said. He looked at White Bear, who had not said anything. He did not have to, for long ago he had counciled for killing every white man who broke the word of their big chief that no more miners would cross the mountains.

White Bear had never changed his mind, but so far he had obeyed the Arrow.

Shavano heaved up from his bone back rest and came to the group. He was as tall as White Bear, a wide man, with the hard, fierce freedom of the mountains stamped on him. On the war chief's broad face White Bear read all the things that he himself believed. Shavano was a fighter. His courage was like a rock. He knew that the coming of the white miners was like water creeping through the grass, just a sparkle of it showing here and there, until all at once the eye realized that all the land was flooded.

Shavano was no coward. He hated white men. But Shavano did not know what to do. True, he had counciled war, but every time the Arrow said not war, but talk.

"The council will begin soon," the war chief said.

Jingling Thunder grunted gloomily.

"Old men talk," Red Cow said. "They talk and more white men cross the mountains. That is council."

Soldier spat. "The war trail is the answer to all talk?"

Shavano's eyes flared dangerously. "When did Shavano turn from the war trail? When did Shavano show fear?"

"Never," White Bear said quietly. He looked at Red Cow and Soldier, shaking his head. He felt as they did, but this was not a thing to be helped by fighting among themselves.

Shavano stalked toward the Arrow's lodge. Little children scrambled from his path. The women were silent as he passed.

CHAPTER 2
White Man's Talk

WHITE BEAR SAT FAR BACK AT THE COUNCIL BEFORE
the Arrow's lodge. As a sub chief of the Uncom-
pahgres, he was entitled to a forward position,
but he did not care to be any closer to the two
white men than necessary. One of them was a
soldier, tall and brown as a plains Indian. Menzies was his name. He had ridden into the camp
without fear. There was no hair on his face.

The second was a big man who had got from
his saddle stiffly, with the water and color of
the sun on his face. He had thick hair down the
sides of his face and hair upon his upper lip.
Although he wore no clothes to mark him as a
soldier, it was said that he was a chief above
Menzies. He was called Shallow.

White Bear sat straight, with the sun heavy
on his back. There would be much talk, like

wind in the aspen leaves, before anything was said. He watched the Arrow.

Like White Bear, the Arrow was not all Ute. His mother had been an Apache, and the Arrow had spent many years in the south among the Spanish whites, so that he knew their language, as well as some talk of the whites who came from the grassy plains. Wide as a rock, hard as a thick pinion tree, the Arrow sat with his sharp eyes watching everyone.

The soldier Menzies was speaking formal words of greeting to the council, talking slowly, stopping to think at times; but he knew the words. When he sat down he spoke in his own language to Shallow, telling what he had said. Shallow smiled a little, and then he rose to speak.

White Bear did not like his voice from the first, although he did not understand the words. Shallow was not giving counsel; he was making threats. He punched with his fingers. They were fat and white. His voice was too sharp and loud. It reminded White Bear too much of other white men's voices on a night long ago.

Greasy Grass translated. He was half Sioux, half white, and had trapped many years in the mountains among the Utes.

"Kill no more white-faces," Greasy Grass said. "Follow the Arrow's way: point them from the country and let them go in peace. The white chief promises that soon no more will cross the mountains." The interpreter swept his hand toward the Continental Divide.

"Soon!" Shavano grunted like a bear.

There had been one promise that the white men would stop crossing the first range of mountains. They had not stopped, and now they were crossing the second range to the sacred hunting grounds of the Utes.

"Arrow will be chief of all the Utes—"

There were startled grunts from many. The Arrow was a sub chief only because the Utes willed it. Who was saying he would be chief of all?

"Only with the Arrow will the white chief make his treaties. Soon the Arrow will go with his sub chiefs to put his name on the talking leaves that will tell what part of the mountains belongs to the Utes and what part to the white chief."

White Bear was stunned. Since the first sun all the mountains had belonged to his people. In astonishment he looked at the Arrow, who was undisturbed. Shavano's face was like a black rock. Jingling Thunder, old warrior that he was, had put one hand over his mouth in surprise.

"There will be meat and presents for the Utes," Greasy Grass went on. "For all the land they once owned there will be payment made every year. It will be done with the Arrow."

The Arrow sat. He said nothing. He did not seem displeased. He had known of this talk in his lodge before the council, White Bear thought. He had agreed to it, and he was only a sub chief. No man among the Utes had the right to give away their land.

But the Arrow did not speak.

"But first," Greasy Grass went on, "those who killed the three white men by the Crooked River two moons ago must come forward. They must be punished."

"By the whites?" Shavano asked.

The interpreter looked at Shallow and spoke. Shallow nodded. He said many words.

Greasy Grass said only, "Yes, by the white men."

White Bear knew who had killed the three miners on Crooked River. Red Cow and Soldier and some other young men. It had been a fair fight. The white men had guns, and the Utes bows and arrows; and so Red Cow and the others had crept in at dawn and killed the white men before they could use their guns. Yes, it had been a fair fight. Soldier and another Ute had been wounded by the white men's knives before the fight was over.

The Utes had not gone into the camp as friends, eaten the white men's food, and then killed them.

When no one spoke or moved, the one called Shallow rose with anger on his face. He started speaking again in his sharp, threatening voice, pointing with his finger.

It was too much. White Bear rose. The speaker stopped, his finger in midair.

"The messenger from the white chief says the Utes who killed three white men must be punished." There was mighty anger in White Bear, but he spoke carefully. "Thirteen summers ago white men killed my family. They also must be punished."

An angry storm came down on the Arrow's face.

Shallow turned to Greasy Grass, who translated White Bear's words. Shallow shook his head, and when his words came from the mouth of Greasy Grass they said, "That was a very long time ago."

"Two moons, thirteen summers. Time does not matter. The white men must also be punished."

There were many grunts of approval, the young men making most of the noise.

The Arrow rose, his face like thunder. "The white brothers come in peace," he said, looking at White Bear. "There must be peace."

The Arrow was not afraid, White Bear knew. Like Shavano, the Arrow did not want peace because he feared war. But the Arrow must know that the mouths of white men ran on and on, while their hands reached for knives. That he must know; but the white man had spoken of making him chief of all the Utes, and perhaps that had caused his eyes to go blind. Perhaps the Arrow had been blind for a long time, ever since he talked to white men alone in his lodge with the sides rolled down to earth when the sun was hot.

"Let the white men give to us for punishment those who killed my family," White Bear said. "Then we can give to him those who killed the men on Crooked River."

Menzies smiled just slightly as he looked at Shallow, who let his words run hard and quickly.

"That cannot be done," the interpreter said.

White Bear grunted scornfully. It was as he had thought. He pointed. "Let all white men stay beyond the mountains."

"My brother is angry," the Arrow said. "White Bear thinks of long ago when bad men came into the country of the Utes and harmed his family. Now the white chief has promised—"

"Let his promises be done, not made by marks on the talking leaves. I have had enough of talking leaves that no one but the white chief understands."

The Arrow's anger rose murderously. He had killed when anger was upon him like that, and now he would have fought with White Bear, but they were too far apart.

"I am the chief!" the Arrow said.

"Ai!" White Bear smiled. "The white man's chief, not mine."

The Arrow sprang forward, drawing his knife as he came. The council was in an uproar instantly. Shavano and Querno grabbed the Arrow, and some of the other sub chiefs helped. Jingling Thunder pushed White Bear back, scowling fiercely.

"The council is no place for fighting," he said.

"Talk. White man's talk." White Bear turned and walked away. From the hill where they had been watching, Soldier, Red Cow and some of the younger men came down to follow White Bear toward his lodge.

Menzies and Shallow marked well their going.

The Arrow was still talking in council when White Bear and his party rode away. They took with them no more than they needed for the war trail.

"Where?" Red Cow asked.

"We will find the white men who slipped back across the mountains," White Bear said.

Soldier grunted happily. He felt the buckskin bag that held his war paint.

* * *

Munro Shallow, special representative of the Commissioner of Indian Affairs, and Captain David Menzies, rode from the camp with Greasy Grass the next morning.

"It didn't take too well," Menzies said.

"It will. The Arrow has to see that it does. He's bought."

Menzies squinted at the rocky pass ahead. "I wouldn't say that exactly."

"Call it anything you want. We set him up as chief of all the Utes. The government deals only through him. He gets an annuity. Ten thousand a year would be cheap just to have someone in authority with whom we can raise hell when it's necessary to our policy." Shallow laughed. "He'll be lucky if he gets a thousand a year."

"What is the policy?"

"Simple. We've known ever since Baker came out of the San Juan that the country is lousy with gold and silver. There'll be a treaty that says everything the other side of the Continental Divide is Ute land, inviolate." Shallow shook his head. "It won't stick, Menzies. It didn't in the Black Hills, and it won't here, and when it starts to slip we'll have the Arrow under our thumb. In a way, it's better than fighting, which is about all those black brutes seem cut out for."

"You think one man can control all the scattered bands of Utes? The Arrow's only a sub chief anyway."

"We'll build him up as the chief. There'll be trouble, yes; but we picked the right man. He thinks well of himself." Shallow looked sidewise at the captain. "How would you like being a major-general, Captain?"

"All right."

"Of course, but maybe not as well as the Arrow will enjoy being the big boss of the Utes."

Captain Menzies kept one eye on Greasy Grass and the other on the country ahead. The half-breed was a first class scout, but Menzies liked to use his own eyes and judgment. And he had not forgotten the young Utes who had walked away from the council with White Bear.

Shallow rode heavily. The country meant nothing to him other than land to cross. He said, "In time we may even convince the Arrow that he's a great, smart chief who foresaw the futility of fighting the white man. Once he has that idea, once he's taken our gifts, he'll have to go right down the line with us."

"Who's 'us'—the Department of Indian—?"

"It's a little more personal than that, Captain. I also represent a group interested in the development of mining in the San Juan."

"You'll help make a treaty that you know our side will break?"

"It's inevitable, Menzies. How many men would you need to keep prospectors out of these mountains?"

Menzies twisted in his McClellan to look at the long caravan of gray-topped peaks running from the mountain of the snow woman. His eyes rested briefly and coldly on Shallow. "Not men, Shallow—corps."

"Exactly. One day the Utes will have to go. In the meantime it would be expensive to fight them, and it would be impossible to keep prospectors and miners from crossing to where they know gold lies."

"Expensive to whom—the mining interests you mentioned?"

Shallow nodded, his face hardening. "And to the government too."

"Which worries you most, Shallow?"

The red-faced man spoke quietly. "How old are you, Captain?"

"Thirty-eight."

"Brevet?"

Menzies nodded curtly.

"I can understand, I was a brigadier at your age."

"A lot of politicians were, fighting the Mexicans from desks in Washington."

Shallow's color deepened. "No need for us to get personal," he said. "No need at all."

They followed Greasy Grass into the first turning of red, sun-scorched rocks that marked the pass.

"What would you do with the Utes, Menzies— let them hunt and fish and camp for the next hundred years on some of the greatest mineral deposits in the world?"

"I don't know; but whatever I did, it wouldn't be with my mind on one thing and my tongue on another. That White Bear hit it when he said promises should be done, not marked on paper."

"White Bear and those other young whelps who walked out on the meeting are setting themselves against big trouble. I spoke to the Arrow privately about them."

"I know," Menzies said. "And the Arrow spoke

privately to me about the last party Red Youman took into the San Juan. The Utes chased
them out, but the Arrow knows the party
started back three days ago." Menzies watched
Shallow carefully. "Where do you suppose
White Bear and those other fire-eaters were going?"

Shallow stopped his horse. "My God! If they
get Red—!" He urged his horse forward again.
"We've got to get word to the colonel!"

"Indian country over there, Shallow. Theirs
by solemn treaty. Enter at your own risk, and
the cavalry won't help you. Youman knows that.
You knew it too—when you sent him to map
out mining claims that your outfit intends to
snatch fast when the Utes have been chased and
butchered."

Shallow was not surprised. "How'd *you* know
I sent Youman?"

"Both I and the colonel have suspected it for
sometime—your plan, I mean. You never heard
of Youman yesterday when I mentioned his
name. Today you call him 'Red' and nearly fall
off your horse when it dawns on you that he
might be gobbled up by Utes. I hope to hell they
get him."

"That's fine talk for a white man, an army of-
ficer."

"Those with him—well, that's too bad, but
they knew their risks. Red Youman deserves
any Ute arrow that catches him. From what I've
put together I think it was he who wiped out
White Bear's family a good many years back."

Shallow was not impressed. He was not even
listening. "It will be serious if they get Youman," he said, half to himself.

Captain Menzies went on ahead to ride beside Greasy Grass. The interpreter had never been known to wash. One eye drooped evilly from an old knife cut that ran from his forehead to his chin. Sometimes he rode all day with no more talking than an occasional grunt.

Menzies preferred him to Munro Shallow.

CHAPTER 3
"Go Now. Ride Far."

TWELVE WARRIORS RODE AWAY WITH WHITE BEAR. When they all knew where they were going, two of them who were nephews of the Arrow stopped the group for council. White Bear was sick of council but he listened.

Sick Wolf, one of the nephews, said it was not good to fight the white man. "Let us war, instead, upon the Arapahoes," he said. "There is always one or two lodges not far from the Waters of the Great Spirit."

Soldier grunted and made the sign of cowardice. From the time of the first mountain the Utes and their plains enemies forgot all thoughts of fighting when they went to drink the waters of Manitou.

"The lodges of these Tattooed Breasts are not *at* the healing waters," Sick Wolf argued. "Only close by."

"You have been too long listening to your uncle, the Arrow," White Bear said. "Go fight the old sick men of the Arapahoes. We ride against the white men."

Red Cow laughed full in Sick Wolf's face and made the sign of cowardice.

Sick Wolf and his brother put their hands upon their knives, but they were afraid of Jingling Thunder's sons, so they only held their hands upon their knives and swore their hatred with their eyes.

"Go back," White Bear said. "Perhaps the Arrow can get his white brothers to help you fight the sick ones at Manitou."

The Arrow's nephews rode away, and with them went another whose heart was not strong.

White Bear was silent a long time as he led the war party up the pass that would take them to the Crooked River. He had made bitter enemies this day, both in council at the camp and just now. Making enemies among one's own people was not good; it held the cloudy thought of what would happen if the Arrow's friendship for white men caused little divisions among all the Mountain Indians, so that they could not stand together when they finally learned they all must fight or lose everything to the water already creeping through the grass.

They stopped on the top of the pass and put on the green and red stripes of their war paint.

There were fifteen mounted white men in the party, with five animals that wore the iron moccasins. It made White Bear's heart sick to see how well they knew the country of the Crooked River, going the easy way, avoiding the bogs and little blind canyons where even Utes who did not know the country well sometimes had trouble.

Straight down the Crooked River they had gone, then turned at the right place in the sage, so that they would miss the big tumbling canyon where no pony could cross. They were going straight and fast for the snowy Spanish Mountains where others before them had washed the yellow stones from the rivers and dug the little holes among the rocks.

Scouting the old camps carefully, White Bear and Soldier saw with what keenness the sites had been chosen, where there was natural protection for the horses, yet two or three ways to escape, and still good cover to fight behind if the attacking force was large. They saw, too, where the guards had been posted, not drowsing by a big fire, but in the rocks and trees on four sides of the camps.

"He who leads these white men is not here the first time," Soldier said. He glanced at his horn bow. "They will all have guns."

There was not a gun in White Bear's party.

"Ai. And they are fifteen and we are ten," White Bear said carelessly. "When their camp is made, they are strong. When they are traveling their scouts will be like eagles. But when they are making their camp, their minds will be on food and rest and other things."

Soldier nodded. "I am with you, brother."

"They will camp this night at the bright lake of the black rocks. We will be there first. From what we have seen, they will send their scouts ahead, then all around the place of camping while their fires are being made."

"You are wise like the coyote and the spider."

"Jorno and Saguache move like smoke against the clouds. Their arrows find the big rabbit of the plains in mid leap. They will wait for the scouts."

"We will fight the rest from the trees and rocks around their camping place?" Soldier asked.

"We will rush on foot into their camp."

Soldier looked thoughtful, but after some time he said, "I am with you, brother."

It was as White Bear had said. The white men prepared to make camp that evening among black rocks in a little open space beside the lake. White Bear and seven young men were watching from the dark spruce trees. They could not spare a man to tend the ponies which had been left behind them in the trees.

Red Cow's black eyes glittered as he crouched with his bow before him, watching the big horses that carried the packs. It would be fun to kill the white men, but riding into camp with two of those large horses behind him would be better.

Soldier watched all movements of the white men. Three of them went to the lake to water the riding ponies, and they did not take their guns. A huge man with sunset in his hairy face sat on a rock and directed the others. He kept his gun across his knees. He would be a bad one, Soldier thought, one they must kill very soon.

Soldier glanced at White Bear, whose face was set like a stone in winter. Until now, Soldier thought, he had not known how much White Bear hated white men.

Two scouts had gone ahead. Jorno and Sa-

guache were waiting somewhere up the lake.
There would be no signal when their work was
done. They were to come back quickly then and
help the others.

The three at the lake were almost ready to
come back. Two of the pack horses were unbur-
dened now, and a man sent them toward water
with slaps upon their rumps. But he did not go
with them, and the three at the lake would return soon and be near their guns. Did not White
Bear see that? Soldier thought.

White Bear had seen. But his mind was reaching far back to the days of He Cries, when he
had crouched at a lodge flap watching a hairy
face whose eyes looked red down the barrel of
a rifle. Out there on the rock with the rifle
across his knees was the same man. White Bear
looked at the rest. He could not tell about them.
It had been long ago, and only one of the five
who had killed his family had become fixed in
his mind.

The red one must be killed very soon in the
fighting.

At the lake the three horse handlers started
their ponies toward the camp.

"No war cries at first," White Bear said, and
sprang from cover.

It was a queer thing, like a dream, White Bear
thought, because for several long racing leaps
the white men did not see the dark bodies
charging at them. Then one of the men at the
lake saw. He yelled.

All the white men busy in the camp looked
toward him, and cost themselves another three
long leaps toward death; but the big one on the

rock did not look at the man who yelled. He looked instinctively toward the trees. He fired the first shot without rising, and off to the left White Bear, from the corner of his eye, saw someone strike the ground.

Then the Utes were on the camp.

Three white men were down in the first hard-driving whisking of the arrows.

Two of the three at the lake leaped on ponies and rode away. The third ran hard toward camp, drawing a long knife as he came. Red Cow killed him with his second arrow.

Straight for the red one White Bear sprang. The man was like a weasel in his quickness. He put a rock between himself and White Bear. His rifle made a sharp chattering noise. Then it threw its thunder again, so close to White Bear that its hot breath burned between his arm and breast.

White Bear struck with his knife, reaching hard, but the red one was out of the way once more. The knife swept down and broke upon the rock. White Bear heard the rifle chatter. It would speak again. He leaped over the rock and caught the warm, round barrel with both hands.

He was strong, with the shoulders and tallness of his Cheyenne heritage, but he could not take the gun from the red one. They were close to each other for a moment, their muscles rigid. White Bear saw the same big white teeth and the same reddish lights in the eyes of the man who would have killed him years before.

White Bear tried to twist the rifle down. It went down a little. Then he reversed his power and tried to whirl it from the red one's hand. But the man was wise, and his arms were like the butts of dried lodge poles. He was too strong.

Suddenly he let White Bear have the rifle, shoving it at him and letting it go, so that the Ute sprawled clear over the rock and fell upon his back. The red one snatched a short gun from his belt and raised it, and the white wings of death made their beating sounds in White Bear's ears.

The hatchet came from somewhere behind White Bear. It rang upon the short gun in the red one's hand. It knocked it from his grasp. The hatchet struck so hard against the man's breast that he should have fallen. But he only let out a great bite of air, then turned and ran like an elk.

"I am with you, brother. Are you hurt?" It was Soldier reaching down to help White Bear.

The air was gone from White Bear. There was blood upon his chest and a gray burn under his arm, but he was not hurt. He got up quickly, in time to see the red one leap upon one of the big horses and gallop down the lake shore.

Saguache and Jorno came sweeping by on their ponies. They yelled that they had killed the scouts with two arrows, and then they rode fast down the lake after the white men who had got away.

There were five of them, counting the red one. Two of them still had rifles. One of them killed Jorno's pony with one shot, so Saguache turned and went back to him, and the two of them came back to the scene of the fight.

Red Cow was dead. He had fought well, the others said; but before the fight was over he had run to catch one of the big horses, and a white man had shot him in the head. Running Wolf was badly wounded. It was he who had fallen at the red one's first shot. No one else was hurt bad. They had come upon the camp so quickly, not shouting war cries, that they had caught the white men by surprise.

It was a great victory. But Red Cow was dead, so it was not a great victory after all, White Bear thought. And the red one had escaped.

Jorno and Saguache were gathering up the white men's ponies. Scattered on the ground and among the packs were many things, among them guns and the sound-making dirt that was used to make the guns speak thunder. Soldier brought the red one's gun to White Bear, and with it small shiny things with soft stone in the ends. Soldier had seen such guns far south among the Spanish whites, and said he knew how to make them speak.

But he would not try tonight. His heart was heavy because of Red Cow. He went around the darkening water, and they saw him climbing upward in the rocks to make his medicine to the spirits of the sky and of the earth. He would tell them of his brother.

They camped at the upper end of the lake. Long after the moon was gone White Bear sat alone by the fire. Soldier came then, bringing a small deer he had killed with an arrow in the moonlight at the edge of the lake. They roasted meat on sticks, not speaking. Saguache, whose stomach was always empty, was wakened by the smell and joined them.

"It was a great victory," he said.

Soldier said, "When the sun comes, I take Red

Cow to the summer camp. It will not be good
when Jingling Thunder knows."

"Bad," White Bear agreed.

A voice came ghostly from the night, so that
Saguache dropped his meat into the ashes and
stood up trembling.

"Jingling Thunder knows," the voice said.

Little drops of winter touched White Bear's
back muscles even after he knew it was his uncle who had spoken. Then Jingling Thunder
came from the dark into the firelight as silently
as the-bird-that-has-no-nest.

After a while White Bear gathered his wits
enough to offer his uncle meat. Jingling Thunder squatted by the fire, eating rapidly. When
that was done, he wiped his hands in his hair
and said, "Querno comes with twenty warriors
to bring the young men back to camp. The Arrow is angry. His nephews spoke of this with a
forked tongue. Shavano would not lead the
party the Arrow sent."

White Bear said with heavy heart, "Now it is
no longer talk. The Arrow fights on the white
man's side."

Jingling Thunder looked old and tired for a
moment. "Rouse the young men. Let them eat
and go farther toward the sunset place. I will
stay here with the wounded one and Red Cow."

White Bear called the others from sleep. They
began to roast meat, blinking at Jingling Thunder.

"After you left the council it was said by the
white man with hair upon his face that it is their
chief's order that the sunset side of the mountains belong to the Utes. The other side is

theirs." There was bitterness on Jingling Thunder's face.

Soldier said angrily, "We did not agree! All the Utes must agree!"

"They will agree through the Arrow," Jingling Thunder said. He stared at the fire, and added, "Perhaps in time the Arrow will see what we see now." His words were without strength, White Bear knew, because his uncle did not believe them himself.

"Do not kill white men who will go from our land," Jingling Thunder said. "Warn them first. Kill them only if they do not heed the warning."

"They are like Arapahoes," White Bear said. "They need no warning when they come into the mountains!"

"The white chief does not care if we kill the Tattooed Breasts," Jingling Thunder said, "or if they kill us." He rose to his full height, and looked sternly at White Bear. "Warn the white men first."

He was wise. He was not afraid. White Bear loved him, and so White Bear said, "We will warn them."

"Go now," Jingling Thunder said. "Ride far."

The young men were ready to leave as soon as they were on their feet. Some were still chewing meat. Others thrust parts of the deer into their breech clouts.

Jingling Thunder's last words made them look away from each other for shame. "In camp, even after victory there must always be sleepless ones to see that no one walks to the fire without being seen or heard."

Jingling Thunder did not look at them again, or watch them go.

CHAPTER 4
They Used the Guns

THAT SUMMER WHITE BEAR'S BAND KEPT THE SPANish Mountains clean of white men. They ranged from the edge of the desert where the rivers became sand to the red waters of the Colorow. They were hard and lean. They moved by night as well as day. In a land of much meat they often did not stop for their bellies when on the trail of white men. Querno could not catch them.

Always, as White Bear had promised, they gave one warning. If their words were heeded and the white-faces started back across the mountains, the band trailed them to see if they were honest.

Sometimes the white-faces lied and tried to steal back to where they had been digging, after they made a pretense of leaving.

All but one of these last left their bones

among the rocks or in the dark gloom of the forests. He who escaped was a big man with no hair on his face. He was like the white bear of the rocks in his fighting, using his arms like clubs after his gun was broken. At last he ran into the rocks where ponies could not follow, going so fast that Jorno, who was lean and like the smoke in lightness of his running, could not catch him.

"Perhaps it was well," Jorno said, after he returned winded.

High up in the rocks the white man paused to laugh and shout back insults in Ute. Ai, he was a brave man, and in a way he reminded White Bear of the soldier called Menzies.

When those who dug the holes and played in the sands of the streams did not take the warning, they died. White Bear taught his band to attack in the night, creeping in close and using only knives. They wiped out several camps that way, and some they cleaned out by killing the white men one by one when they grew too excited over their digging and wandered away from each other in the day time.

None of the band, not even Soldier, cared much for the night fighting, although White Bear said many times that none of them had been wounded that way, while several of them had been hurt in day attacks.

They did not use their guns until late in the summer. They were afraid, because the first time Saguache tried to shoot his rifle it knocked him over and made a terrible sound. Saguache ran in a circle for a while, holding his hands over his head. The barrel of the rifle had a split in it, like a drum skin that had been stretched too tight when wet.

Soldier, who was wise about guns, said the white men had put a curse on them, but that it would pass before the leaves fell. It was better not to use the guns until he was sure the evil spirit was gone from them.

The evil spirit left not very long afterward when they met a Spanish trader on the Piedra. Soldier made much talk with him about the guns, and had the trader examine all the rifles. Afterward, Soldier said the curse was gone, that they must not let dirt or mud get in the barrels of the guns, and that they must be kept clean by means of the cloth and iron stick he had stolen from the trader.

"I think you should have been a medicine man," White Bear told his friend.

They used the guns on one party of stubborn white men not far from the dusty cliff ruins of the Old Ones. There were four white men. The band killed them all while they were running toward their camp. White Bear thought he killed two of them, because his rifle was a many-shooting one. He shot several times more than anyone else, but he counted coup on only one white man.

White Bear had eight scalps that summer.

Ai, the band kept the Spanish Mountains clear of the diggers. White Bear thought they had done well, especially since they had to hide from Querno's warriors who had come to take them back to camp, as well as search out white men.

Sick Wolf and Little Buffalo, the Arrow's

nephews, were with Querno and they worked harder than any to find the band. And one day Little Buffalo did.

He called to them one evening when they were camped without fire on the Animas. He was on the other bank of the river, out of sight in tall grass.

"It is Little Buffalo," he said. "I have looked for you."

White Bear's band was moving away, spreading out in the gloom. They knew where to meet later.

"I am alone," Little Buffalo said. "I want to speak to White Bear."

It might be a trap. White Bear made the night bird signals for his band to keep on going. He stayed where he was.

"Come," he called to Little Buffalo.

Soon the Arrow's nephew came dripping from the river. White Bear let him wait in the darkness until he was sure no others were swimming behind him, and then he spoke softly, and Little Buffalo walked to him.

"You have done well this summer."

White Bear was silent.

"Running Wolf's wound grows well. He is almost strong again."

White Bear said nothing.

"The council was with Jingling Thunder. The Arrow was afraid to try to punish him for warning White Bear's warriors."

That was glad news, but White Bear was silent.

"The Arrow has gone with many sub chiefs to the far lodge of the great white soldier to talk of a treaty." Little Buffalo was growing angry. He stood there and would say no more.

"Why do you come?" White Bear asked at last.

Little Buffalo was sullen. He waited long before answering. "I come to join White Bear. My heart is with him."

White Bear considered long. "We do not need Little Buffalo, or his brother Sick Wolf."

Little Buffalo took a deep, hard breath of anger.

From the darkness close by came Soldier's voice. "They turned back once. They would turn back again at a worse time."

"Go, Little Buffalo," White Bear said.

So angry that he stumbled and made great noise at the edge of the water, Little Buffalo went away.

Soldier and White Bear went silently to join the rest of the band. This place by the Animas was unclean. They would not stay the night.

"He was an enemy once. Now he is a great enemy," Soldier said.

It was so, White Bear thought.

When the leaves were dying on the trembling trees, Running Wolf came to find them. They saw him from afar and knew who he was, but for three days they played with him, letting him almost find them, then slipping away. He knew they were there, but he would not call out to them even when he knew they were close and watching him.

Running Wolf played the game.

Then one day on the Villecito he built a great fire in a sand pit by the water and roasted whole a fat buck. The smell of it came back into the trees where the band was watching. They had not suffered from hunger, but it had been long since they had seen a feast like that.

Saguache's stomach began to make bear noises. The others laughed, but they were licking their lips.

"We have played long enough," White Bear said.

They joined Running Wolf then. He seemed surprised to see them, and asked where they had been all summer. "If my brothers are hungry, there is a little meat."

Ai, they were hungry. Quivera and Twin Buck were the first to throw the meat from their teeth and wash their mouths with water. White Bear held his face without expression and kept eating long after he knew the roasted buck had been smeared with the leaves of the bitter-stink plant, so that not even a starving Arapahoe could have eaten it. At last, when his nose and stomach could no longer stand it, he ran for the river.

Running Wolf whooped.

They rolled Running Wolf in the sand, and then they threw him in the river. He was well recovered from the wound the red one had given him at the lake of the black rocks, for he took Soldier and Twin Buck into the water with him.

It was good to have Running Wolf with them again.

Saguache found the second deer hidden in the trees. It was even fatter than the first, and not foul from bitter-stink leaves. They had a feast and much good talk of what had happened that summer, and Saguache fell asleep in the middle of boasting of the white-faces he had killed.

But as always the fear of what was happening to the Utes came back to them.

"The Arrow and the other chiefs have returned from the great white lodge," Running Wolf said. "The Arrow now wears a shirt like the white-faces. They brought back many presents."

"Did they put marks upon the talking leaves?" White Bear asked.

"Even Shavano. The talking leaves say now that all across the mountains is the white man's, even the big park where the buffalo were once like the grass in numbers."

"And no more white-faces will come across the mountains?" Soldier asked.

"They say it," Running Wolf said. "The bad voice called Shallow, who returned with the Arrow, said it before the council."

"Who believes it?" White Bear asked.

"Not Jingling Thunder," Running Wolf said. "Not Shavano. Shavano sits much with clouds upon his face, and sometimes will not talk, even to the Arrow."

"Shavano made his mark upon the talking leaves. That means nothing. Let him council war, instead of sitting in silence in his lodge," White Bear said.

"The war chief is wise," Running Wolf said. "He is not afraid of white-faces, but perhaps he sees things in his medicine that we do not see."

"Shavano is old," Jorno said. "That is all. There were eight of us this summer. We made the white-faces fear to stay on this side of the mountains. Let Shavano come to our help with all the Utes who are not afraid and the white-faces cannot send an army across the mountains. Let the Arrow stay with his white brothers and wear their clothes."

It was good talk, true talk. But White Bear was uneasy. Even in the warm sun of the falling leaves a bad spirit came to him, and gave him a little chill like the snowbird walking on his grave. It was very bad that the Utes were divided, worse that on the side of the white-faces was a wise and powerful chief like the Arrow. White Bear was a little afraid of the Arrow, and he knew it.

"One day the Arrow will kill Jingling Thunder, like he did Red Shirt and Bad Nose when they stood against him," Running Wolf said somberly. "Jingling Thunder speaks openly against what the Arrow is doing."

"Then I will kill the Arrow," Soldier said.

"And then the white-faces will say that Little Buffalo or Sick Wolf is chief of all the Utes, and that they will make their talk only through one of them." Running Wolf shook his head.

It was a bad thing to think about. It made them all cloudy of face, except Saguache, who had wakened and was eating again. It was even too much to hold in the head, so that night they moved again and went in search of white men.

Over one range of mountains at the hot waters near the booming rocks, they found a camp of six white-faces who had built a little lodge of logs near where they had been digging in the mountain.

The band crept down through the trees to watch. One of them was careless, making a small noise or showing himself, because a white man came from behind the log lodge where he had been watching, and made the signs of peace, even though he could not see them then.

It was the same huge white-face who had fought them like a bear before he escaped.

Soldier raised his rifle carefully.

"No," White Bear said. "He knows the old signs. I will talk to him."

"He was warned to go away once," Soldier said. "I will kill him."

White Bear pushed Soldier's rifle down. "There are others with him. He is a brave one, even if he is a white-face."

"Soon you will be like the Arrow," Soldier said angrily.

It was well that he was White Bear's great friend, but even so White Bear was still trembling with anger when he went down alone to talk to the white-face. The man knew all the signs, and he spoke White Bear's language without hesitation.

"I am Big Buffalo."

"I am White Bear."

"Big Buffalo's party will stay here till the new leaves come. The Arrow has said it. Your uncle, Jingling Thunder, was beside him when the Arrow said it. Jingling Thunder did not like it, but he sent this to make it true."

The white man took a ring from a pouch of his clothing and held it out.

It was Jingling Thunder's ring, stripped from the finger of a Navajo in a fight before White Bear was born. White Bear did not stare too long. He tried to keep the sickness from his face. The Arrow's word to all white men was different from his word to one white man, for then a chief's promise was the promise of all Utes with good hearts.

White Bear was confused. He did not know what to say.

"I will take council," he said, and turned back toward the hill.

He was almost to the trees when Big Buffalo shouted. White Bear turned his head to look. He saw in the door of the log lodge the red one he hated, and the red one had a rifle in his hands, already raised. It spoke while Big Buffalo was springing toward him.

White Bear's head became full of the sky. He knew no more.

On great wings White Bear came down and down until all was black; and then he soared again, and his head was full of noises of the old spirits of the mountains talking to him. He was dead, and his friends had put him in the rocks without his pony or his weapons. And now he could not ride or hunt.

Then the spirits went away and his eyes were seeing other things. He was on dead leaves in a camp. Soldier was there with him. From somewhere there came the sound of rifles.

"I am with you, brother," Soldier said. "White Bear went far toward the great hunting grounds in the sky, but now he is back once more."

White Bear listened to the rifles.

"We are killing the white-faces?"

"We are trying," Soldier said. "For three suns we have tried, but they are strong fighters and wise. They fight from their wooden lodge. We cannot reach them, and last night the one called

Big Buffalo slipped away in the darkness. We have tried to roll the mountain down upon their lodge, but it is near a ledge and our stones bounce high and go over it."

White Bear sat up. His head was loose upon his neck, and there was a tear along the side where the red one's bullet had passed.

Big Buffalo would go to the Arrow. It was best to kill the other white men as quickly as possible. White Bear did not feel like killing anything at the moment, but he got up, holding to a tree.

Killing the white men proved very difficult. The logs of their lodge were green and large and stopped bullets. The roof was of dirt. As Soldier said, rocks rolled down the mountain always struck the ledge and bounded clear beyond the lodge, which was built with one corner over a little spring.

Big Buffalo himself must have selected the site, White Bear thought.

On the second day after he came from his sleep, White Bear took his men away. Before they faded into the mountains they saw the dust of a large band of the Arrow's warriors on a far ridge in the valley. Ai, the Arrow was truly on the side of the white-faces now!

The band spent the winter among their brothers on the White River. Old Broken Knife, the chief, treated them with honor, and the young men treated them as great warriors.

Soldier admitted that they were great warriors, and made free with the unmarried women.

Several times the Arrow sent messengers to Broken Knife, with word to hold the band for punishment, but each time the scouts knew in advance, and White Bear was warned, so that he could take his warriors away. And then Broken Knife had his own young men search furiously for them until the messengers were gone.

When the spring grass came and the ponies began to get the looseness from their bellies, White Bear married Gray Bird, the youngest daughter of Broken Knife. Broken Knife had held out long for White Bear to marry his oldest daughter, Wind Eater, who had a sharp, prying voice and not much roundness to her body, but in the end he grunted that young men were all alike, and gave Gray Bird to White Bear.

By then Soldier and Jorno had returned from the San Juan with the cache of white men's rifles and ammunition hidden the summer before. Broken Knife was happy.

White Bear was happy, too, although he soon discovered that, while Gray Bird's voice was not as sharp as her sister's, it was just as prying. But she was a joy in the lodge, and her mother had taught her well about the things a warrior must have in his stomach.

CHAPTER 5
Big Fire at Night

ALMOST FIFTY YOUNG MEN WANTED TO GO WITH White Bear and the others that summer. White Bear did not want so many, but he could not well refuse, and so the young Utes made ready once more to kill all white men who crossed the mountains and who would not take the warning to leave.

Then Jingling Thunder came to the White River camp.

He looked as if the winter had sat heavy on him and brought him many years all at once.

"The Arrow's heart has changed toward White Bear and the other young men," Jingling Thunder said.

There had been long ceremonies and greetings with Broken Knife and the other chiefs, but now White Bear and Soldier had Jingling Thunder in White Bear's lodge.

Gray Bird left quietly to visit with the women when she saw there would be much smoking and serious talk.

Jingling Thunder watched her go with wise eyes. "Will there be a son in the month of deep snows?" he asked.

White Bear said he did not know.

Jingling Thunder's eyes twinkled. "Which, then, of Broken Knife's young men does know?"

Soldier rolled on his robes with laughing.

Jesting went soon from Jingling Thunder's eyes. "The Arrow has changed his heart toward White Bear's band. There will be no punishment. The Arrow sends word to return to his camp."

"What changed his heart?" White Bear asked.

Jingling Thunder smoked slowly. "Perhaps knowing that many young men are anxious to follow White Bear now. How can the Arrow be chief of all the Utes if his young men do not obey?" He passed the pipe to White Bear.

"Should we obey, my father?" White Bear asked.

Jingling Thunder's eyes went far away. They saw the old campfires of the Black Indians. They saw the buffalo on the great hunting park now lost. They saw many things; and they came back to the lodge old and troubled.

"What you have done is well. You held your promise to warn all white men. The one called Rickey—Big Buffalo—spoke with a true tongue about the fight at booming rocks, and of the first time you sent him from the Ute country." Jingling Thunder was silent for a long time. White Bear passed the pipe to Soldier.

"The one with the red hairy face—Youman—

spoke with the forked tongue. Now I wish I had
killed him when he rode past me the evening of
the fight at the lake of the black rocks; but I lay
hidden in the rocks and let him and the others go."

"Your arrow would have been good," White
Bear said. "He is the one who killed Big Elk
long ago."

Jingling Thunder turned his head slowly.
"You are sure?"

"I am sure."

Soldier grunted. White Bear had never said
before why he hated the red one so much.

Jingling Thunder stored the thought somewhere deep inside him, saying no more of it.
"White Bear and my other son have killed many
whitefaces. I do not speak against it, but can
you drink the waters from the rivers, or gather
all the fallen leaves from the trembling trees?"

"We can kill those who come across the
mountains," Soldier said, passing the pipe
around to his father.

"They will come again," White Bear said.
"They are like the ones with madness in their
heads when they see the yellow stones."

"Ai," Jingling Thunder said. "They will not
stop. I have counciled war against them. Only
to White Bear and Soldier have I spoken the
thoughts that come to me when the lodge is
dark; can we hold them from crossing the
mountains?"

Soldier rose and made the death signs with
his hands. "Let all the Utes fight together and
even those who wear the striped pants and
carry the long knives at their sides cannot cross
the mountains."

For a time the clouds left Jingling Thunder's face and he was a fierce, hard warrior; but the doubt returned and he let the pipe go cold in his mouth. "Many follow the Arrow," he said.

"We do not," White Bear said. "We will not go back."

"When I was very young," Jingling Thunder said, "my friends argued about what a bear does in his den. We did not know. To find out Jingling Thunder crawled into a den to see what the bear did."

White Bear and Soldier looked sidewise at each other. Jingling Thunder rose and left the lodge.

And so it was that White Bear, taking his wife, led the band back toward the summer camp of the Arrow a few suns after Jingling Thunder left. With them went more than forty of Broken Knife's young men, not interested in knowing what the bear did in his den, but hoping there would be fighting against the white man later in the summer.

White Bear led them the long way, taking time to look upon all the places where the white-faces had dug the summer before. They did not find a white man in the country.

Broken Knife's young men, already proving hard to handle, were disappointed.

This time the Arrow's camp was at the old place below *Puerta de Pocha* in what by treaty was white man's country. On the way, Soldier and White Bear cast hard looks at seeing many log lodges built in green valleys since the summer before. The tame, skinny cattle of the white-faces were already on the land.

"When the new white-faces hear of the tall

grasses of the Crooked River . . ." Soldier said, and was then grimly silent.

The camp was like a bubbling pot when scouts brought the news that White Bear's band was returning. Young men came racing out on their ponies. They looked with envy on the scalps that White Bear's warriors wore.

White Bear and the others rode into camp with their faces straight, as if they were returning from a little hunting trip. The maidens watched them boldly. Children bounded across the grass to run beside their ponies. The chiefs watched without expression.

Sick Wolf and Little Buffalo sat beside their uncle's lodge with their faces dark, and the Arrow did not come from his lodge at all, like a chief who is too great to look on small things.

Big Shavano, the war chief, came to White Bear before he was dismounted. "It is better not to show so freely the scalps of the white man," Shavano said, while his eyes were counting.

Soldier said, "I do not see the shirt of the white-faces on your back. Is it on your words?"

The thunder of his rage rolled behind Shavano's eyes. "You are on the wrong side of the mountains with your scalps."

"Your mark on the talking leaves helped make it so," Jorno said. "Where are your presents from the white chief?"

Shavano reached to pull Jorno from his pony, but White Bear was quick and sent his pinto between them, speaking to Jorno, saying to Shavano, "You are right, Shavano. We will put the scalps from sight."

The war chief stalked away.

The incident put a little cloud upon White Bear's return.

Big Buffalo, the white man, came from the Arrow's lodge, grinning when he saw White Bear's band. He came to them, his face changing a little when he saw the scalps, but his signs and words were good.

"White Bear and his brothers are good fighters."

"You are fast among the rocks," Jorno said, and laughed.

Big Buffalo laughed, too. "It is well that I was, Streak-in-the-sky."

Jorno considered the name. He liked it.

"I was not fast enough to stop Youman from firing at your back, White Bear," Big Buffalo said. "I did not like that."

White Bear smiled. "Did White Bear like it?" And then he thought that he was making friends with a white-face, so he put his features back in stern cast and rode away; but Jorno and Saguache stayed longer to talk to Big Buffalo.

The Arrow waited three days before he called the council. White Bear's band had the word of Jingling Thunder that there would be no punishment, but the Arrow let them wait.

Under many skins that turned the weeping sky the council was held by a big fire at night.

It seemed to White Bear that there was a little fat upon the Arrow now, as on one who sits in the lodge too much, not riding to make war or hunt. But the Arrow's face was the same, hard and watchful, with the same old wiseness. Ai, it was hard to tell about the bear, even after crawling into his den.

The Arrow talked much, doing almost all the

talking. He was getting like the white-faces, who did not know that there must be long waiting and ceremony, even when there was little to say.

"Our young men have returned from the war trail," the Arrow said. "It is well. We will need them soon."

Now even the children at the edge of the willows were listening, but the Arrow did not at once continue with his thought. "White Bear's warriors have kept the white men from the Spanish Mountains. The Arrow did not like the way it was done, but it is done, and there will be no punishment. Now the great white chief has said that no more of his people will cross the mountains."

Soldier started to speak, but his father jabbed him in the ribs with his elbow.

"In the month of falling leaves the Arrow said that the white man, Big Buffalo, and his party could stay the winter in Ute land. It may be so again with others if the Arrow says. We do not want the rocks of the mountains; we do not want the yellow stones of the rivers. So that there may be peace the Arrow will sometimes let white men go to see about these worthless stones.

"Our young men—" the Arrow looked hard at White Bear's band—"must leave those few white men to dig in peace."

"A few!" Soldier muttered. "They will be like the fish of a beaver pond in numbers. They will build their log lodges, kill the game—"

Sick Wolf tapped Soldier lightly with a club. With him was Little Buffalo and others of the police that saw there was order at council. In the old days those with clubs rarely had anything to do but drowse in the darkness beyond the firelight, but now White Bear saw that there were many of them.

But still a man had a right to speak in council. After a while White Bear would speak.

The Arrow went on and on. He used his own name much. He did not, as in other days, pause to ask advice of the other chiefs and the old men. But his words ran out at last.

White Bear rose to speak. Before he could say anything the Arrow was talking once more.

"I am glad White Bear and his band have returned with so many strong warriors from our brother, Broken Knife. We go at tomorrow's sun to fight a great band of the Tattooed Breasts who have come into the mountains to kill our game."

White Bear never had a chance to speak. There were grunts and much shouting, with preparations for a war dance being made at once.

With his face gleaming like the black stones of the booming rocks, old Jingling Thunder said, "Many days ago the Arrow knew about the Arapahoes. He knew when they were in a place where we could have caught them in the rocks, and Shavano wanted to. But the Arrow waits until he could use them to keep you silent."

"I will not go to fight the Arapahoes," White Bear said.

"Soldier will not go either."

After the camp was roaring with preparations for the war dance, White Bear sat looking at the fire. Rain was falling through the smoke hole in the hides above. Little by little it would make ashes of the bright flames in time.

The fire was the Ute Indians. The little drops coming steadily were the white-faces.

Both Soldier and White Bear went to fight the

Tattooed Breasts. They had to, for the young
men clamored for them to go, Saguache, Twin
Buck, Jorno and the rest adding their voices.
How could White Bear expect Arrow's people
and the others to follow him against the white-
faces later if it seemed he was afraid to fight
Arapahoes now?

Shavano led. He did not like it because the
Arrow had used his knowing of the Arapahoes
to get his way in council, meanwhile letting Tattooed Ones move freely. Even though the treaty
of the talking leaves said this was white-face land
now, still the Arapahoes had no right to be here.

Jingling Thunder said gloomily, "The white
man do not care if the Indians kill each other.
If they all killed each other, the white-faces
would be pleased."

He was so long of face that Soldier laughed
at him, but Jingling Thunder did not laugh.

They rode in one day to where the scouts were
watching the Arapahoes. It was not a good place
for attack. To start, it was a place of ghosts, at
the hill where the Utes had killed a large party
of Spanish miners many far years ago. There in
the rocks was still buried the muleskin bags of
yellow stones and dirt the Spanish miners had
been carrying with them.

Then, the hill was like an old buffalo bull
driven from the herd, all by itself on a flat place
by the river, but close enough to the hills behind it so that the Arapahoes hunting back there
had come out quickly before the Utes arrived.

Shavano scowled, and White Bear knew his
thoughts; warriors could not creep upon the
Arapahoe camp, because there was only flat-

ness all around the hill there on the other side of the river.

The Arapahoes rode back and forth upon their ponies, waving lances that bore Ute scalps, shouting insults across the river. There were more than a hundred in their camp.

"The Coyote leads them," Shavano said. "I would like to catch him in the rocks some day."

"We had the chance," Jingling Thunder said, "but the Arrow waited. Now?"

"First, we will let the wild young men grow tired, so they will listen later," Shavano said.

Hot young warriors had already crossed the river farther up, among them most of those who had come with White Bear from Broken Knife's camp. They rode down on the Arapahoes in a great cloud of dust, some firing arrows and guns before they were in range.

Coyote came streaking out and counted coup with his stick on a Ute, then spun his pinto and went back untouched.

Except for that no one went too close. The Arapahoes raced their ponies and fired their guns and arrows and made great dust. The Ute young men did the same, but no one got too close. And no one on either side was hurt.

Shavano got from his pony, sat on a rock and smoked.

The Arrow and Big Buffalo rode up together to watch.

CHAPTER 6
A Good Plan

TOWARD EVENING, WHEN MOST OF THE YOUNG UTES had come back across the river to eat and boast, White Bear and his band crossed over. Most of the Arapahoes were in their camp by then, eating and resting.

White Bear took his men straight at the scouts on the north side of the hill. Four times White Bear fired his many-shooting guns, but he still had bullets left. Soldier and the others did not fire at all. They merely whooped and made big clouds of dust smoke with their ponies.

When it was time to turn back at the safe place, the Utes did not turn. They went in faster, no longer whooping, their rifles ready. The fifteen Arapahoe guards were caught by surprise. Their ponies were tired. They had not expected anything like this on the first day of battle.

Before they realized, the Utes were very close to them, not trying to count coup, just coming in to kill them. White Bear's band rode right through them, killing two. They did not stop even then. Straight at the Arapahoe camp they rode.

The Tattooed Breasts leaped up from their cooking fires, spilling their meat in the sand, shouting angrily as they ran toward their ponies. And then White Bear turned his warriors and rode toward the high bank of the river. They slid their ponies down through the rolling white stones, crossed the river, and rode up the other bank. Arrows whacked among the choke cherry bushes, and bullets dug into the rolling stones.

White Bear's band got up the bank and out of range.

It was a great victory, and the joke was greater yet, for they had caused the Arapahoes to become excited like squaws.

All the Ute young men rode back and forth on their side of the river and shouted insults. The Tattooed Breasts returned to their cooking fires, this time leaving many guards around their camp.

Even Shavano smiled a little. "Ai, that was good."

"It was good," the Arrow said, but he did not smile.

That night some of the Coyote's men stole across the river and killed a Ute scout and got away.

The fighting would last about three days, Jingling Thunder said. By then the Arapahoes would have had enough and be ready to leave; and the Utes would be ready to let them go.

White Bear went to Shavano with his plan. The war chief listened well, and said, "It is a way to be killed."

"It is a way to make a great victory."

Shavano thought a long time. "We will try it."

When the sun was high the next day White Bear and his band, with twenty picked young men, crept up under the high bank from far down river, where they had gone the night before. It would not have done to go by darkness directly under the bank before the Arapahoe camp, because the Tattooed Breasts would scout in the morning to see that no Utes were hiding there.

White Bear was almost in position. From the flats above he heard the shouting and the noise where the Utes were riding in force all around the hill, keeping the enemy busy. The plan was for White Bear's warriors to rush on foot through the camp and gain the rocks behind. They would cut loose the spare ponies hidden there, then be able to fire upon the Arapahoes from their own fort.

Shavano's two large groups of warriors on the flats would close in on the north and south. The fighting would be broken then, the Arapahoes scattering; and since the Utes outnumbered them almost three to one, there should be a great killing of Tattooed Breasts.

Like smoke from a lake in morning, two Arapahoes rose from the willows ahead, so close that White Bear could see the pigment of their war paint.

Jorno, who never left his bow behind even when he had his rifle, shot one of the Arapahoes through the throat. Saguache got the other with an arrow in the chest, then ran and killed him while the Arapahoe was struggling up the bank. The warrior had shouted, but not loud enough to be heard on the flats above.

White Bear took his young men in a rush over the bank. The new ones made loud war shouts at once, although White Bear had said not to do so until they were seen. It made little difference, for they were seen at once. Like the wind they ran to catch up with Jorno, who was far ahead in a short time.

Eight or nine Arapahoes who had been circling the hill came at them on their ponies. The Utes killed three of the ponies, not stopping to kill one of the riders who had been thrown and could not rise. The other Tattooed Breasts picked up their unhorsed brothers and split away, going toward the flanks of the hill for help.

Shavano's two groups feinted mighty charges, keeping most of the Arapahoes busy. And so it was White Bear's band that rushed into the camp. They found three wounded and two warriors who were trying to make a broken rifle work again. In seconds the Utes cut them dead and rushed on up the hill, where they cut loose and stampeded fifteen horses that a boy was guarding.

The young boy could have escaped, but he tried to fight. His orangewood bow was too big for him. It was clumsy in the rocks. Twin Buck killed him with a bullet.

"We have won!" Soldier shouted.

White Bear looked from the rocks, now that there was time. They had much to do yet, and nobody had won. On the north he saw Shavano trying hard to make his warriors close on the Tattooed Breasts. Shavano was doing well.

On the south the other mounted Utes were holding back, making feints, but not riding too close. White Bear saw Sick Wolf's big buckskin, and after a while he saw Little Buffalo's *grulla* pony; and in a moment he could tell from the way the warriors acted that the Arrow's nephews were leading the second group.

Ai, that was bad. The Arrow himself must have ordered Shavano to let his nephews lead. Shavano would have sent Jingling Thunder, or Querno—or a good fighter.

Groups of Arapahoes began to break off from those opposing Sick Wolf and the others. They came back toward the hill. Arapahoes from the east side of the hill began to come down through the rocks. White Bear's men were busy soon.

Shavano made great charges, sometimes driving those before him almost to the hill before having to turn back. But the Tattooed Breasts came in from the west side now. They were no longer scattered, and they were hard to fight, as always.

Still the Arrow's nephews did not press hard. They made a show. They rode and fired their guns and shot their arrows. From across the river it would seem that they were doing well, but from where White Bear was, they were not doing well. Unless their leaders took them in, the warriors could not be expected to go within knife distance of their enemies.

The Tattooed Ones soon saw they were not facing good leaders on the south. Many of them rode back to the hill, and began to creep up through the rocks. Soon Sick Wolf and his brother were being held off by half their number.

White Bear's band was being smothered, the Arapahoes firing now from all sides. Twin Buck was killed through the head when he rose to fire. Three others were dead.

Through the swirl of dust on the flats White Bear saw Jingling Thunder racing toward Sick Wolf's warriors, with Arapahoes trying to catch him. Jingling Thunder's pony was good. The old Ute reached Sick Wolf, sitting high on his pony, waving his rifle, trying to get Sick Wolf to lead a good charge.

Sick Wolf would not do it. He wanted to council. This, White Bear could tell from the hill, although he heard nothing but the guns of the Arapahoes around him, and the bubbling of Quivera, who was dying with a bullet in the stomach and an arrow in the chest.

Jingling Thunder led a charge himself, with some of Sick Wolf's warriors following him, farther toward the hill than any had gone before from the south. The young men turned back when two were shot from their ponies.

Jingling Thunder did not turn back. He rode into the Arapahoes, striking with the rifle Soldier had given him, clearing a way. He went through and to the hill, and then he rode his pony up the hill as far as the rocks would let him. And then he ran with the Tattooed Breasts rising around him.

White Bear, Soldier and Jorno went to help.

The White Wings brushed them. Soldier killed a chief with his own knife. White Bear used his rifle like a war maul, and Jorno—Streak-in-the-sky—was many places at once, striking with his knife. The Arapahoes had caught a great bear in Jingling Thunder. He came through them with an arrow in his thigh, and bleeding on the arms where knives had struck him. With those who came to help him, he reached the place where White Bear's group was growing smaller.

When Jingling Thunder had air to speak, he said, "White Bear's men must go back. Sick Wolf and his brother will not fight, and Shavano cannot fight on two sides of the hill at once."

It was so, and White Bear knew it.

Shavano knew it too. He led all his warriors in a brave charge clear to the foot of the hill when he saw White Bear's group retreating, and before him he drove some of the Arapahoe ponies that had scattered on the flats. Fleet Jorno caught one, and then he rode and grabbed the war rope of another, and whirled it back to Jingling Thunder.

It was all dust and shouting.

White Bear was knocked without wind by a pony that ran wildly. Soldier picked him from the ground. "I am with you, brother."

The Utes who had rushed the hill went back to the river, some on ponies they had caught, some still on foot. Soldier and White Bear had to go on foot, dodging Arapahoes and Utes alike. In the dust and noise it was hard to tell what was going on.

Running Wolf was wounded again. Saguache

was knocked without sense by an Arapahoe lance, but Tomichi carried him away.

And still the Arrow's nephews did not lead their warriors in to help, although some of the young men came by themselves and fought well.

It was enough. The Arapahoes took their dead and began to ride back into the hills. Some of the young Utes followed, hoping there would be stragglers, which there never were when the Tattooed Ones retreated from Ute country.

Soldier and White Bear, their wounds still bleeding, the dust still in their teeth, went to find Sick Wolf and Little Buffalo. They called the Arrow's nephews cowards, and pulled them from their ponies and would have killed them; but Shavano was there. With the help of other chiefs he separated the struggling fighters.

"Enough are dead," he said.

The Utes had lost almost twenty warriors. They had killed more than that number of the Arapahoes, but it was not a great victory as it should have been, and there would be terrible wailing of the women in the Ute camp on return.

Sick Wolf and Little Buffalo got up from the dust where Soldier and White Bear had left them gasping for wind.

"It was a foolish plan that White Bear made," Little Buffalo said. "He gave us many dead because of it."

The chiefs had a hard time holding White Bear.

On the slow ride back to the camp among the cottonwoods at *Puerta de Pocha*, the Arrow looked sidewise at White Bear and said, "Ai, it was a foolish plan."

"It was a good plan," Shavano said. He looked full at Sick Wolf and Little Buffalo, both unwounded.

The Arrow did not say more, but his face was full of thinking as he glanced again at White Bear and Soldier.

White Bear was more wounded than he thought. It was many suns before he felt like riding on the war trail again. Many young men wanted to follow him now. Every day scouts rode in to say that white-faces were crossing the mountains all the time, more and more of them.

The Arrow said that he would make talk with the messenger of the white chief soon about this thing.

And then the soldiers came up the valley with the cattle, presents for the Utes. Riding at the head was the soldier Menzies.

White Bear's insides became rocks and his brain screamed with rage when he saw who rode beside Menzies. The hairy-face called Shallow—and the red one. The Arrow came and stood before White Bear.

"They come in peace. Remember well, White Bear. The Arrow says it."

White Bear turned away without speaking. Sick Wolf and Little Buffalo were looking at him with hatred in their eyes.

"Does White Bear go away because he fears the one called Youman will knock him over a rock again and take the knife from his hand?" Little Buffalo jeered.

White Bear made ready to leave the camp. Tomorrow he would return to the war trail against

the white-faces, sending Gray Bird to her father, taking with him only Soldier, Jorno, Saguache, Running Wolf, Tomichi, and Wounded
Bull—those who had made the band the summer before. Quivera and Twin Buck were dead.

Jingling Thunder came to the lodge where
White Bear sat staring at a cold fire pit. Gray
Bird looked at the old Ute's face and went away
quietly.

"The white man's cattle are lean," Jingling
Thunder said. "They are like the deer that has
long carried an arrow in his belly. Some of them
could not even live to get here."

"White man's presents."

"Ai." Jingling Thunder smoked. "The red one
talks much to the Arrow. He talks of taking not
one but many parties across the mountains. The
Arrow waits. He had made promises to Big Buffalo about the same thing, and the one called
Youman is angry."

"Let the red one wait," White Bear said.
"Soon the Arrow will tell all white-faces to cross
the mountains."

Jingling Thunder looked around the lodge and
saw the signs of moving: "You go?"

"I go."

"Jingling Thunder will go with you. It is time
for even the old ones to fight the white-faces
beyond the sunset mountains. Jingling Thunder
has seen the white man's presents, and they are
like his work—lean and worthless."

White Bear's heart was glad. He said gravely,
"My father is welcome. He has the strength and
wisdom of ten warriors."

Jingling Thunder passed the pipe. "We cannot kill the red one here."

"He will cross the mountains again. The heavy stones have put a madness in him."

Jingling Thunder sat with folded arms. "The white one called Big Buffalo—he is brave. His heart is good."

"If he comes alone across the mountains it is well. If he brings many white-faces with him, he is like the rest and must be killed."

They smoked until the pipe was dead.

White Bear went about the camp, quietly telling his band that they would leave when the next sun came. He looked at the cattle, and they were as Jingling Thunder had said, not good for Arapahoe squaws to eat. He saw Menzies and the soldiers. They were camped apart from the Utes.

He was passing the Arrow's lodge when Big Buffalo came from it. And then from behind the lodge the red one came with anger on his face. He made strong words with Big Buffalo. White Bear did not know what they were, but they came from anger, and the red one used the Arrow's name often.

Big Buffalo only grinned and started away. The red one grabbed his shoulder. Like the white bear of the rocks, Big Buffalo turned. His arm pointed quickly and hard, with the fingers closed. The hand went into the red one's hairy face and knocked him to the ground. He rose with his white teeth showing.

Big Buffalo's other hand pointed and the red one sat down once more. He grabbed at the short gun in his belt. Big Buffalo had one in his hand first. He spoke soft words to the red one, who got up very angry and went into the Arrow's lodge.

Big Buffalo closed one eye and grinned at White Bear, and went away making a little song. He was a strong fighter, White Bear thought, but he should have killed the red one there on the ground. Then White Bear was glad it was not so, for he was going to kill the red one someday, even if old Jingling Thunder thought *he* was going to.

Before there was light someone brought White Bear from his robes with scratching on the lodge flaps. It was Jingling Thunder who came in before the words were said.

"Big Buffalo is dead. Your knife is in his heart. Go now."

"I did not kill Big Buffalo. Someone took my knife from the lodge while the council met last night."

"It is so, but Sick Wolf has seen the knife. He has told Menzies and Shallow and the Arrow. They met. Shallow said Menzies must have his soldiers take you away. The Arrow agreed."

White Bear's heart was sick. "I did not kill Big Buffalo."

"Go now!"

"How do you know this thing?"

Jingling Thunder listened at the tent flap, then looked into the dark. White Bear could hear movement at the soldier camp.

"Menzies sent Greasy Grass to tell me, so I could tell White Bear. Both Menzies and Greasy Grass think that the red one killed Big Buffalo, but Shallow says the soldiers must take White Bear. And the Arrow sees the chance to have the white-faces hang by the neck one who stands across his path."

Ai, it was clear enough to White Bear.

They could hear the soldiers coming. Menzies had sent the warning; he could do no more now.

White Bear grabbed his rifle and went under the hides at the back of the lodge, running in the darkness toward the herd of ponies.

He heard Shallow shouting in his sharp voice. He heard the soldier Menzies, and later, the red one yelled something in the white-face tongue. Rifles crashed against the night, but no one was shooting at White Bear.

He thought of Jingling Thunder and Gray Bird left in the lodge, and would have raced back, but Soldier came out of the darkness with two ponies.

"We must ride far," Soldier said, and threw the hair rope over White Bear's arm.

Behind them the camp was in an uproar.

They rode toward the sunset mountains. Never again, White Bear vowed, would he come on the side of the rocks that the white-faces owned.

CHAPTER 7
With No Warning

CAPTAIN MENZIES DRANK SIX CUPS OF COFFEE FOR breakfast. He paced his tent in a cold rage. His men had killed two Utes.

Munro Shallow sat smoking a cigar, smiling to himself. "Sit down, Captain. No harm is done that the Arrow can't patch up. What's two dead Indians?"

"You know as well as I, Shallow, that Red Youman put that knife in Bill Rickey while he was asleep. They had a fight last night over Rickey getting the edge about going into the San Juan. Youman worked with Sick Wolf and that other nephew of the Arrow's. One of them got the knife for Youman."

"Maybe the Arrow didn't know about it—my guess is he didn't—"

"You're making a *lot* of guesses, Captain."

Shallow lifted the coffee pot. "My God, have you drunk all of it?"

"—the Arrow didn't know about it at first, but you can bet he does now. But he's satisfied. White Bear was giving him trouble. Jingling Thunder was in his way. Now White Bear is an outlaw and Jingling Thunder is dead."

"You should have better control over your men, Menzies," Shallow said blandly. "Shooting White Bear's squaw . . ."

Menzies turned, gray-faced with anger. He looked a long time at Shallow, so long that red began to creep alongside the man's thick sideburns.

"Shallow, Red Youman rattled those four green recruits into firing blindly into that tent, and you know it. In fact, if I had my way, I'd hang Red Youman, and hold you responsible for framing this whole thing."

"Be careful, Menzies. In the first place, you don't have the power. In the second place, you don't have the connections to be even hinting that to me. Put it in your report of this affair—and see what happens to those bars." Shallow rolled his cigar slowly across his tight mouth. His eyes were cold and venomous.

"Don't forget, too, in your report, to mention that your men were so poorly controlled they fired when a civilian yelled that White Bear was coming out with a knife. And don't forget to mention who sent Jingling Thunder to warn that lop-eared Indian. It was Greasy Grass. Who sent Greasy Grass to tell Jingling Thunder?" Shallow laughed softly. "You sort of put yourself over a barrel, Captain."

Menzies' hands were clenched into the sides

of his trousers. His face had gone from gray to white, so that the blackness of his brows was startling. His speech was a trifle slurred.

"Shallow, you're the filthiest kind of slimy thing this country has to put up with. You use the Army to do your dirty work. You don't care how many troopers or how many Indians kill each other in the process, so long as each death helps you get to that gold in the San Juan. You had Bill Rickey killed, or at least you knew about it.

"There'll be probably fifty white men killed in the San Juan because of what you did in this camp last night, but you and your kind are so stinking rotten you don't care so long as it brings the day closer when the Army will have to move in and fight the Utes."

Shallow rose. "If you perform as well as you talk, Captain, it will be a relief to have you protecting my miners in the San Juan—that is, if the Army hasn't thrown you out by then."

Captain Menzies moved without haste. He spun Shallow around, with one hand in the collar of the man's black coat, the other clutching the seat of Shallow's trousers. He threw him through the tent door with such force that Shallow rolled over and over until he was in the ashes of a cooking fire at the feet of a startled sergeant.

Soldier and White Bear were camped at the old place in the valley of purple grass when Tomichi and Wounded Bull found them, bringing news that Jingling Thunder and Gray Bird were dead.

"The Arapahoes could not kill Jingling Thunder," Tomichi said. "The white-faces killed him while he stood without weapons in your lodge, White Bear."

Soldier and White Bear went separate ways into the rocks. They would not show grief, even to each other.

That night the band crept in upon a camp of white-face diggers in a deep canyon by the water. Four men were sleeping on the ground, and the band killed them quickly, without much noise. But there was a cave they had not known about, the mouth of it hidden by high willows.

Two rifles sent thunder from it, Tomichi went down with a heavy grunt. The rifles spoke so fast the rest of the band had to scatter, unable to take their brother with them.

When the light came they saw Tomichi on the ground beside the dead white men, with blood on his chest. He was not dead, for his eyes moved a little and he saw White Bear and Soldier and Wounded Bull hiding in the bushes above the cave.

It was a long wait. The sun came down into the deep canyon before a white man left the cave. White Bear put his hand on Soldier's rifle. After a while the second white-face left the cave. The Utes wounded them both, so that they were easily killed.

Tomichi was dead by then. It was a poor victory.

Now the band was only three. The white-faces who had crossed the mountains this summer were in much larger groups than before. They stayed closer together, even when they dug, keeping their rifles with them always. But still, they sometimes grew careless. The band killed four more of them, catching careless ones in four different camps.

The white-faces were everywhere this summer, with more coming day by day. White Bear remembered Jingling Thunder's gloomy words spoken in the camp of Broken Knife, *Can we keep them from crossing the mountains?*

One day the band found a camp of ten whites that had been wiped out by Utes. Later, they found Bad Jack, a chief of the Northern Utes, with his party of twenty-five young men. Bad Jack, too, had enough of white-face promises.

It was good, and White Bear felt better; but he did not stay with Bad Jack, whose young men were noisy fighters, staying in the rocks and trees, closing in on a camp only when all the white-faces in it were wounded.

Again the Arrow sent Querno with many fighters to bring the warring Utes from their path. Mostly Querno tried to catch Bad Jack, whose party was large.

But Querno did not catch anyone. Half of his young men left him and went with Bad Jack.

Jorno, Saguache, and Running Wolf joined the band at the camp of the smoking rock. White Bear had wondered why they were so long in coming.

"The soldier Menzies has come again to the Arrow's camp with many cattle," Jorno said. "This time they were good cattle. Menzies said he knew they were not good last time. The Utes chased the cattle and killed them like buffalo, letting them go one at a time."

Saguache shook his head. "It was not like killing buffalo. It was not good sport."

Running Wolf, who limped from his wound

at Spanish Hill, said gloomily, "The buffalo are gone from our big park of grass."

It would always be "our park," White Bear thought, no matter what the talking leaves said.

"Even on the plains the buffalo are almost gone now," said Running Wolf.

They were silent for a long time.

"The soldier Menzies knows you did not kill Big Buffalo, White Bear," Jorno said. He looked at Saguache. "He knows the red one did it, but he cannot kill the one called Youman because the white-face Shallow says the word of Utes is not good."

"It was the red one who made the young soldiers fire when Jingling Thunder and Gray Bird were killed," Saguache said. "But still Shallow took the red one away and would not let Menzies do anything."

"How does Menzies know this thing?" White Bear asked.

Jorno, Saguache and Running Wolf smiled at each other.

"Sick Wolf said the words, telling that Little Buffalo stole White Bear's knife and gave it to the red one."

White Bear stared.

"Sick Wolf and Little Buffalo went hunting," Jorno said. "It happened that we hunted in the same place that day. Sick Wolf's ears were gone when we took him to talk to Menzies afterward. Little Buffalo could not talk at all."

"He was dead," White Bear said.

Jorno shook his head. "He was truly a forked tongue. We did it with his own knife."

"It was better than killing him," Running

Wolf said. "Now he will be known until the last sunset as one who is a liar and a coward."

"What did the Arrow—?" Wounded Bull asked.

"The Arrow was gone to get more clothes and worthless presents from his white brothers." Saguache yawned. "I am hungry. Do my brothers have meat in this camp, or must Running Wolf roast another buck?"

Ai, the band was a scourge that summer, ranging far, striking silently. As in White Bear's first attack since his return, they gave no warning. The promise had been made to Jingling Thunder, and he was dead, and he had been killed by white-faces without warning.

Bad Jack's warriors were very busy too. Others came down from the Northern Utes. Some skinny Paiutes from the big red river came to help. They were not very strong fighters, but they helped put fear into the white-faces. Young men slipped from the Arrow's camp and crossed the mountains. All of them wanted to join White Bear's band but he did not want a large force, so he took only Cocho Querno's son, who was a silent fighter.

Querno gave up in disgust and went back to the Arrow's camp. Only six men went back with him. The rest were fighting the white-faces in little bands of their own.

Before the torch of fall touched the leaves of the trembling trees, the white-faces had again been driven from Ute country. It could be that way always, White Bear thought, if the Utes would fight as they had this summer.

CHAPTER 8
The Red One

A STILL, HEAVY HEAT LAY ON THE SAN LUIS VAL-
ley, and it seemed to Captain Menzies that Fort
Garland was the focus point of it, with Colonel
Rowland Oder's office the very needle point itself.

Menzies pulled his shirt away from his chest
and looked through the door at the cool sum-
mits of the *Sangre de Cristo* Mountains. He had
been too long in the Army to complain of heat
or cold or anything that could not be controlled—and a lot of things that could have been
controlled.

Colonel Oder handed him the order. It was
from the President himself, passed down
through regular channels "*. . . available military
forces in the area . . . proceed at once . . . remove
from Ute Indian lands . . . all miners and other
trespassers . . .*"

Menzies grinned. "At last something makes sense."

"I can spare two troops, Menzies. You'll have trouble, but don't get too rough." Oder wiped his forehead with a soggy handkerchief. "Keep on the lookout for White Bear and Soldier, and bring them in too if you can."

Menzies glanced again at the order. "Even now?"

"The order still stands. Our old friend Munro Shallow has seen to that. Start this afternoon, if you want to." Oder cleared his throat and picked up another paper. "Red Youman is your guide."

Menzies stared.

"Right from the War Department, Captain. It says that Youman knows every diggings in the San Juan. It says that he should prove invaluable in dealing with the miners."

"I don't want him."

"You've got him. You don't know as many politicians as Shallow does. So you'll take him, Menzies." The Colonel smiled briefly. "And you'll bring him back too. It says here that he's 'invaluable'."

Captain Menzies took his two troops past Los Pinos Agency with Red Youman riding at his side. Five hundred Utes loafing at the agency, waiting for rations and gifts that never seemed to come, went wild with joy when they heard the news. They had sold much of their land, and then surveyors told them that they had sold much more than the talking leaves said. There had been councils, arguments, treaties, deals, promises during the last few years.

The Utes discovered that they had not understood the treaties and the deals. The promises were not kept, and those who came to make the treaties always said later that their chief and his big council had changed things. Meanwhile, miners and farmers had kept pushing into the San Juan. Railroads had moved toward the rich basin. Mills had been built.

Only White Bear and a few small bands that fought sporadically had stood against the incursion this last summer. They had not been enough to turn the miners back.

Menzies could understand the feeling of the Utes on hearing that his soldiers were now going to move the miners out.

"A damn' fool order," Youman said. "It'd make more sense if you was going down there to kill every stinking Ute that's been giving honest miners trouble."

High on the gray hills above the Crooked River White Bear sat his pony and watched the soldiers moving in Ute land. Running Wolf was dead now. Wounded Bull was dead. Cocho had gone back to his father, badly wounded in the fighting against the white-faces. Bad Jack had quit, returning to the White River, where there was now a place where food was sometimes given to the Utes, with a white man there to tell them what to do.

Ai, the water had crept through all the grass now. Only White Bear's band and a few others remained. Always the Arrow had given away more land, taken more presents from the white-faces, counciled peace.

The Arrow had put a big knife in the backs of his people.

Now the soldiers had come.

"Shall we fight them?" Soldier spoke without boasting. They were four. Jorno, Saguache, he and White Bear. Soldier saw from one side of his face now. A bullet that slid upon the rocks in a fight the summer before had torn away the corner of his right eye.

"We will fight the soldiers," White Bear said. "Go. Tell all the young men scattered in their summer lodges to gather at the old camping place beyond the bright lake of the black rocks. White Bear will watch the soldiers."

It was the first time White Bear had ever asked for help. It was time. The sun was growing dark over what was left of Ute land.

For two days he watched the soldiers. They moved without haste. On the second day they turned in the gray sage toward the lake of the black rocks. White Bear had been seen, he knew, but it made no difference, for the one who led the striped-pants was Menzies, and he would know that he was being watched.

At the place of the dying elk, when the soldiers were eating, Menzies rode alone toward the hill where White Bear was, making the signs of peace. White Bear did not put down his rifle, and he let Menzies ride clear up the hill to him.

There were no more years on the soldier, it seemed to White Bear. He was as brown and straight as ever. They made all the signs, then sat upon the ground facing each other. Menzies did not use White Bear's name.

"We come to put the miners from the Ute lands."

White Bear thought he had not heard with good ears.

"The great white chief has said it."

"It is time," White Bear said.

Menzies nodded gravely. "When you ride the country, if you see the one called White Bear, tell him that the Arrow and the white chief still are angry with him. Tell White Bear to stay hidden in the mountain. Perhaps in time the anger against him will pass."

"I will tell him," White Bear said.

He watched Menzies ride back to the camp. Why did one who spoke with a true tongue let the red one ride with him? Right now the red one, who had watched with the far-seeing glasses, was shouting at Menzies, pointing toward the hill. He shouted in his anger so loudly that White Bear heard his own name.

Menzies' heart was good, but still the soldiers must be watched to see that it was so about putting the miners from the San Juan. White Bear, who knew all that had happened in many councils, even though he had not been there, knew that the white-faces sent to speak to the Utes said one thing with good heart—and then later their big chiefs claimed another thing had been said.

Ai, it would be well to watch the soldiers.

Before the sun was gone Jorno and Saguache came to say that three hundred fighters would be gathered at the lake of the black rocks that night, almost all of them with guns.

It was hard for White Bear to say, "The soldiers come to make the white-face miners leave our lands. The one called Menzies has said it."

Jorno and Saguache would not believe at first.

"Until we see if this thing is true, we will not fight," White Bear said.

They watched a white soldier coming fast on his horse to catch the troops, now moving across the little valley of many bucks. This last one had come many far miles, for his horse was wobbling. He rode to Menzies and gave him a talking leaf. All the soldiers stopped.

After a while the red one made a great booming sound of laughing that came faintly to White Bear and the others on the hill.

The soldier put their horses out to grass. Presently, Menzies, looking all around, signalled the hill where White Bear was, then rode toward it.

This time White Bear went down to meet him.

Great anger and shame was on the face of Menzies, but he made all the signs, not speaking quickly like an excited squaw.

"The great white chief has changed his mind. We are not to put the miners from the San Juan."

After a while the soldiers rode back the way they had come.

For a long time the three Utes sat on the hill with bitterness eating at their hearts. Then Jorno said, "I will ride to watch the soldiers, to see that they are not tricking us again."

White Bear and Saguache went to the old camping place above the lake of the black rocks. Nearly four hundred warriors were there, and they were ready to fight. Soldier wanted to take them after the striped-pants and kill them all, including Menzies. It made no difference to Soldier that Menzies had been told what to do by his chief.

Many young men grunted in agreement when they heard Soldier's angry speech.

"They go," White Bear said. "Let them go."

"Then they will return to guard the miners someday," Soldier said. "It is better to kill them now."

"Fighting here in the rocks, where we were ready, is not like trying to fight them in the open of the Crooked River," White Bear said. "They will be there before we can catch them." For the first time White Bear wondered gloomily if the Arrow had been right in not wanting to fight the white-faces.

"Something has changed White Bear's heart," Soldier said. "Does he grow afraid?"

"Menzies is taking the striped-pants away," White Bear said. "Let them go."

He and Soldier quarreled bitterly. In the end, Soldier took all who would follow and rode to fight the cavalry. By then many Utes had slipped into the night, their hotness cooling after thinking how it would be to meet the soldiers in the open by the Crooked River. Saguache went with Soldier.

White Bear sat alone. It was like the night when he had sat by the fire thinking of the death of Red Cow; and it was not far from the same place. Faces moved in the flames, Red Cow, Twin Buck, Quivea, Jingling Thunder, Gray Bird, Tomichi, Wounded Bull . . . all gone to the sky . . .

He heard a pony coming. For a while out there in the darkness where he met it, he did not know who it was that had fallen across his moccasins.

Jorno's voice was not strong. White Bear felt

a great hole in his back when he reached to help him.

"At night the red one left the soldiers and went toward the San Juan on the Trail of Stolen Ponies," Jorno said. "I followed to kill him, but he hid beside the trail and killed me instead."

It was so. When White Bear got his brother to the fire he saw that Jorno had not long to live. Ai, this day had brought great blackness.

Jorno was dead when White Bear rode the war trail after the red one. He found the first marks at daylight. Then he saw where the white man had stepped from his horse to a high rock beside the trail, and hidden to shoot Jorno when he came. The horse had gone on up the mountain, then waited in the trees for the red one to mount again. It would be a good horse to own, White Bear thought.

Twice more that day he found where the red one had tried the trick, taking no chances that others besides Jorno had not been following. White Bear would not be caught that way. On the second day he thought he knew where the red one was going, toward the big camp of the white miners in the park of snowy mountains.

White Bear cut wide to the north and rode hard to get ahead. He put many bleeding places on the legs of his pony, but the red one was still ahead when he reached the spring-that-never-stops. White Bear's pony was used up. He changed to Jorno's buckskin, which did not like the extra weight; but it was fleet and strong.

And so on the third evening White Bear caught up with his enemy, who was camped in the rocks in a bad place to get at. He had a small fire that sent little smoke and did not show, but the smell of it came to White Bear, who waited for darkness.

After dark there was still a little fire, which did not fool White Bear. The red one knew he was close. The red one would not be sleeping near that fire.

Very slowly White Bear went in, so well that even the red one's horse did not see or hear or smell him to give an alarm. The fire was almost dead, but it gave enough light for White Bear to see, after some time, a blanket and the stock of a rifle where the red one lay between two rocks some distance from the fire.

Fading back into the darkness, White Bear went around the camp, but not far enough to let the red one's horse catch his smell. He crept in with his knife.

He was close enough.

Too late White Bear learned the trick. The red one was not where the gun and blanket lay. He was beyond, in the blackness near the horse.

The thunder was like the noise that had wakened White Bear long ago when first he heard it. Three times it came. After the first time White Bear was lying flat on his back from a bullet that had smashed his left arm and knocked him over.

Then the red one came from the darkness as one who knows his bullets always go true. But he still had the short gun in his hand and it was ready. White Bear waited while the red one came closer, even then not making any noise.

The Ute's right arm was strong. He threw his knife so that it could not miss. The red one grunted. His gun flamed. By the light of it, while springing up, White Bear saw that his knife had gone too high. It was just under the red one's shoulder, not in his heart. But it had caused the red one to drop his gun even as he fired it.

White Bear went in to put the knife where it belonged.

The white man was like a grizzly. He tore White Bear's good hand from his throat and made the stars come down with blows against his face. He hugged him with big arms and made the bones of White Bear's back cry out. Then White Bear used his legs and knees in the way he had been taught him childhood.

It was good. They went down together with the red one underneath. White Bear felt for his knife, but it had been knocked loose from the red one's shoulder. He tried again to kill the white man's air with his one hand.

Youman rolled with him, and just in time White Bear remembered to keep the roll going. They went over twice, crushing out the fire. White Bear was still on top. Fingers struck his eyes and blinded him. He had to dig his head against the heavy smell of the red one's shirt to keep from losing his eyes.

Grunting curses, Youman came up with his great strength seeming to grow greater. He brought White Bear up with him, held him with one hand, hit him with the other so that all the rocks of the mountain were rolling in White Bear's head.

He held with his hand to the white man's beard and used his legs again. This time the red one crashed backward into a rock and did not fall. But much strength went from him. One hand that had been killing White Bear's wind fell away.

Ai, White Bear had him then, he thought, and tried once more to crack the red one's head against the rock.

The pain in White Bear's side was not great at first, and then the sharpness came again. The red one's hand that had gone from his throat was striking with a knife. White Bear twisted, using his legs once more. This time the red one struck the rock so that he could not move for a moment. It was long enough for White Bear to get his fingers gripped as he wanted them.

He bent his enemy across the rock with his back curving more and more, with Youman's head going lower and lower. And still the red one had great life. He almost broke the hold and flung White Bear back. But now, his strength flowing fast, White Bear was fighting everything bad that had happened to him.

He held on and used his power until a dull snapping told him that it was done.

White Bear fell across the body and could not move for a while. He fell again when he tried to go toward his pony. For a while he crawled toward his pony. Then he could not remember where it was at all. A great blackness came to him.

As once long ago when the red one had shot him in the head, he came down and down and saw the world again. Soldier was squatting beside him.

"I am with you, brother."

White Bear's wounds had been bound with

fresh hide from a pony, but it would not be enough, he knew.

"When is it?" he asked.

"Two suns after you killed the red one."

"He is dead?"

"He is dead," Soldier said.

"You fought the striped-pants?"

"Only a little. Few went all the way with us. We fought them just enough that Saguache was killed. It was too much. We should have heard your words, brother."

"I have few left," White Bear said. "But my eyes are with me yet. Take me high into the rocks."

They came at last to a great tumbled place of gray slabs where the old spirits long ago had thrown stones in mighty anger.

"White Bear will stay here."

Soldier helped him to sit against a rock.

Below them the San Juan was spread with its gleaming rivers and great gray mountains reaching toward the Manitou. They saw the valleys with their rich green grass, the cool forests of trembling trees and dark pines. It seemed to White Bear that it was safe now. It was secure forever and would always be the sacred hunting grounds where the grass never burned away or the game grew scarce.

"Go back to the Arrow's camp," White Bear said. "The land is ours now till the last big sunset, and there will be no more trouble. The red one was the last to go, and it is done now."

"Soldier will go." Soldier knew that White Bear could not see the smoke of white-face fires below them, or the growing scars of those who dug the mountains.

"We fought to be free," White Bear said. "Even if we had lost, it would be well." For a moment his eyes were puzzled and he looked at Soldier with fear. "We have won a great victory. That is true?"

"It is so. The white-faces have been driven from our land forever, White Bear."

After a while White Bear murmured, "Running Woman ... Running Woman, the lodge grows cold ..."

From the mists above the vast San Juan, White Bear's grandmother came toward him smiling. Her buckskins were like the snow, her braids shining like the wetness on the booming rocks; and she was not old.

"It is well, He Cries," she said.

Not long afterward Soldier went from the mountain alone, going toward the Arrow's camp.